KING
of the
PYGMIES

Jonathon Scott Fuqua

CANDLEWICK PRESS
CAMBRIDGE, MASSACHUSETTS

Copyright © 2005 by Jonathon Scott Fuqua

First paperback edition 2007

Library of Congress Cataloging-in-Publication Data is available.

Library of Congress Catalog Card Number 2005050178

ISBN 978-0-7636-1418-8 (hardcover)
ISBN 978-0-7636-3412-4 (paperback)

2 4 6 8 10 9 7 5 3 1

Printed in the United States of America

This book was typeset in Granjon and Universe.

Candlewick Press
2067 Massachusetts Avenue
Cambridge, Massachusetts 02140

visit us at www.candlewick.com

For Calla and Gabriel, who keep me grounded

Chapter One

My hometown of Havre de Grace, Maryland, sits like a caught branch at the end of the Susquehanna River, a giant waterway that churns down from New York State, cuts across Pennsylvania, and pours into the very top of the Chesapeake Bay, which I can see from my bedroom window. The area is green and humid in the summer, but rough and wiry as you'd ever imagine in the wintertime. Havre de Grace is a tough rail town, crisscrossed and chopped up by tracks. About twenty times a day, freight and Amtrak trains rip through, horns blasting before they pass over bridges that fire straight across the broad mouth of the Susquehanna River. It's not the kind of place where miracles happen.

The area where the river ends and the bay starts is so wide open you can watch the weather for an hour before it might hit. As a matter of fact, a few years ago, my older brother and I were caught on the water during a bad storm. Waves and wind whipped up and swamped our boat so that the two of us had to hold tight to the sides till we were hauled out by a fisherman. Momma and Dad were furious at me. They said I had disregarded clear signs of trouble. They were right, too: I'd watched the gray towering clouds for a long while before making the decision to disregard them.

Some things can't be disregarded, like Matty, my older brother. He was born with his umbilical cord twisted tight around his neck, causing him to be retarded. The thing is, he's turned out okay. He's nice and isn't so slow that he can't tell jokes or be serious. He's six years older than me, and mostly he looks it. At twenty-one, he's a lot taller than me, like everyone else. He's also got the rugged, mature face of a movie star. When I was little, we played all the time, and we never stopped hanging out. Now we're like weird friends who are different but still have the best time with each other.

Not so long back, on a Saturday, he and I wandered down to the docks on Congress Avenue, where the combined waters of the bay and the Susquehanna wash against brown pilings that were set in place about fifty years back. As usual, we sat down and swung our legs off the splintery end.

Hoping I'd get a big reaction, I reached into my coat pocket and took out a pack of cigarettes.

Matty stared at me. "What's that for?"

"Just started smoking," I explained, "and I love it. Cigarettes are refreshing and good-tasting and make me feel mature."

"But they're bad for you."

"That's not until you're about ninety, and I don't wanna live that long, anyway. When you're that old, you can't do anything but drool. I'm gonna enjoy myself right now, while I'm young." I lit up and took a puff. "Oh, man, I—I love this tas—" I couldn't finish my comment. I could barely breathe from coughing. To be truthful, it was my first pack of cigarettes ever, and each time I put my lips to one, my stomach churned and I hacked till it felt like my skull was loose on my spine.

"Doesn't seem like you love 'em," Matty told me flatly, peering out in the direction of a far-off sailboat.

"I—I really do," I promised, still coughing. "Don't—don't be fooled, huh."

Without looking my way, Matty declared, "Cigarettes kill people when they're young, not just when they're old, Penn."

Catching my breath, I stared at the tip of my Camel, hesitant to take another puff. "That's called government propaganda. The government's just trying to keep people from enjoying themselves."

"Why do they wanna do that?"

I stared at Matty's handsome face, at the razor stubble halo on his chin. "I don't know."

Matty reached a hand up and called a big, beautiful seagull like it was a dog. "Wish I had some bread," he said.

What I wished was that he wasn't there so that I could get rid of the stupid cigarette without losing face.

I took another suck and coughed so hard my brain hurt. "Damn," I gasped, and as I did, Matty told me how, one day soon, I'd be hooked to about twenty different hospital machines and wheezing air with busted lungs. If that happened, he would scream and wail and his heart would be as broken as anything I could ever imagine, worse than any sort of real pain, like a dislocated finger or a swollen ankle. In fact, if I died, he wouldn't want to live either.

I looked at him. "God, Matty, shut up. You're just upset 'cause I'm starting to enjoy life. You wanna drag me down, is all."

"What?"

"You wouldn't kill yourself. That's bullshit."

He stared at me. "I didn't say that."

4

I scowled. "I'm serious, grow up."

Matty shook his head back and forth. "I didn't say anything to you, Penn. I didn't. I was just thinking and watching the bird."

"Stop," I told him. "Stop doing that."

"What?"

"Stop talking to me with . . . with your mouth closed."

"I'm not."

"You were!" But I could tell he hadn't done it, and I gawked at the cigarette in my hand. Suddenly it was worse than holding a poisonous snake. It was terrifying. I whipped it into the water. Watching it float, I trembled and shook, and a tiredness like I'd never felt before seeped through me. "God, Matty. I heard you. I heard you say that stuff."

"Penn, that's 'cause smoking's like doing drugs. It makes you feel weird."

"You think?" I lowered myself onto my back so that my shoulders rested on the gray wooden boards.

"They got stuff in them," he explained.

"People say they're loaded with chemicals."

"Don't smoke anymore."

"I'm never going to. Not . . . not 'cause you don't like it, either. It's 'cause my brain must not react right to cigarettes or something. I get a bad reaction." Closing my eyes, I struggled to catch my breath.

5

With a finger, Matty brushed at my cheek, causing me to open my eyes. "Penn," he said, "the funny thing is that I would kill myself if you died. It's true. I don't ever want you to leave me."

"Don't worry. I'm not going to," I promised, staring into the blackest clouds I'd ever seen in my life.

In history class, we sat learning about the Great Depression, for about the tenth time since first grade. Every single year, history teachers go over the same stories. There's the Revolutionary War, which comes after the Declaration of Independence. There's George Washington with his wooden teeth, and Thomas Jefferson and his one billion fancy quotes. It goes on and on till George W. Bush becomes president, which is where, I guess, history ends and the present day starts. Anyway, as our teacher was yacking about the Great Depression and how millionaires were throwing themselves out windows, I was wasting my time, as usual, watching Daisy Parra, who I had a crush on.

She was the new girl at school, Chinese, I thought, and ever since I'd seen her, I wanted to be her boyfriend. She was beautiful and sweet-seeming with soft brown cheeks and skin. Also, her puffy lips were perfect, while her big black eyes were magnified by thick glasses. I wanted to give her a hug and tell her secrets.

Sensing my gaze, Daisy glanced over. Embarrassed, I dropped my head and looked at my blank notebook page. I kept my eyes down for a while, then I peered up at the teacher, who was going on about people selling pencils and standing in soup lines. He asked a question, and Daisy answered it. It seemed like she could answer anything. Her voice wasn't foreign, either. It was sweet and soft. The fact is, everything about her, including her flat, pointy shoes and pressed secretary pants got me feeling that way.

When school got out, I passed slowly through a pack of about thirty other kids. A bunch of us went into the Burger King, where my momma and dad first met twenty-five years ago. Getting in a long line behind a mob of classmates and soldiers from the Aberdeen Proving Grounds — this military base down the road that tests the way bombs and missiles explode — I watched Matty, who worked the flame broiler. Right before I ordered, I called, "Hey, Matty, how's it going?"

He looked up and grinned. "I made forty-seven hamburgers so far."

To act amazed, I blew air out of my mouth, then I ordered a large soda.

Outside, the day was cool even though the sun was bright and the sky was smooth and blue. As I walked along Union Avenue, my fingers ached from the cold

Coke, forcing me to switch the cup back and forth a lot. I tromped by pretty houses and two old, expensive bed-and-breakfast hotels that are painted about five different classy colors and kept so that even toothpick wrappers don't litter their yards. Next to one, a mansion was getting rebuilt one piece a year, so that by the time it was new again, the owners would be dying of old age.

In the shadow of Havre de Grace Hospital's parking garage, a crowd of smart students who lived near me caught up and passed. They didn't say anything, and I ignored them. But they seemed to be having such a good time that I wished I was a part of their group.

The wind blew, and a handful of red and yellow leaves floated down from the pretty, wide trees by the roadside. Even though my teeth started chattering, it seemed so nice outside that I imagined holding Daisy's hand and sneaking somewhere to kiss. What I loved about her was how innocent she seemed, while the thing that got me excited in a sexy way was thinking that she might be less innocent around me.

At my house, I dumped my books, checked the answering machine, and got a snack. After sitting for a bit, I grabbed a jacket from my room and headed downtown to pick up my pile of newspapers, the *Havre de Grace Morning Document,* which for some reason comes out in the afternoon. I used to complain to my momma and dad that my newspaper delivery job was too hard for a high school kid. I acted like it was killing me. In fact, unless it's raining or sub-zero out, it's easy. The problem is, it takes a few hours, meaning I can hardly ever hang out with friends in the afternoons. It could be worse. Almost all of my customers are nice, even the poor ones. And, when it comes to the few surly people on my list, I have a way of dealing with them: I get revenge by pounding the paper into their tangled hedges. So that it doesn't seem like I do it on purpose, I keep a calendar in my head, spacing things out.

At the dusty office of the *Havre de Grace Morning Document,* I said hello to Rhonda, the secretary, and grabbed the pile of papers with my name on it. Hauling them out the front door, I sat on the sidewalk rolling them up. About halfway through, I happened to look up and see my uncle Hewitt staggering toward me along Green Street. I turned my head and tried to act busy and in a hurry.

When I was little, I used to like watching my uncle from behind my dad's legs. The reason is, he drinks till he can't talk sometimes, which never stops him from trying. Still, most everyone is friendly with him. In fact, a few times a year, my father visits his falling-to-pieces house to laugh about our wild family.

It was the death of my aunt Birdy, his wife, that

caused him to become a bum. Up until the day he lost her, Uncle Hewitt was Havre de Grace's chief of police. The story was that during his thirty years as an officer, he never drew his pistol. He used his nerves instead. Then Aunt Birdy died, and he quit as the police chief and became the town drunk.

As I busily filled my bag, Uncle Hewitt wandered on down the block and disappeared into a bar named Sturgeon's. Relieved, I finished up and shouldered my bag.

Weaving from block to block, I flung papers and listened to train horns calling in the distance. Overhead, giant military planes curled in toward the Aberdeen Proving Grounds, which is where, I'd heard, Daisy's dad worked. I wondered what kind of job he had and if he spoke any English. I worried that if I ever got to go out with Daisy, Mr. Parra would call me *sir* and bow a thousand times like the Chinese do in movies. If that happened, I decided to be real decent and tell him he could stop bowing and that he should call me by my first name.

On Revolution Street, with its broken-down businesses that look like cow skulls in desert paintings, my friends were hanging out around their favorite spot, the closed Citgo gas station. Like homeless kids, they were seated around the rusty pumps and sandwich board signs with the words scratched out. A week before, they'd convinced me to buy a pack of Camels and try smoking. My cousin Hurlee had explained that cigarettes would make me look more mature, which would cause girls (Daisy, I was hoping) to go crazy for me.

I scuffed over. "Hey."

"What up, homey?" Hurlee asked.

"Delivering papers, like always."

"Wanna cigarette?"

I shook my head. "Naw, man."

"Come on, Penn. Yo."

I straightened the newspaper sack across one of my shoulders. "Dude, one gave me a reaction."

Hurlee scoffed. "A reaction?"

"Yeah, it made me sick."

In a lazy, cool way, he rose from the curb and inspected me like he was looking for something. After about half a minute, he reached over and touched my chest. "I don't see any tiddies, Cuz," he said.

I forced his hand away. "That's 'cause the only tiddy around here is you."

Laughing, he blew out cigarette smoke, and it whirled around his face and wheedled up my nose.

Holding my breath, I hissed, "I gotta get going." I was scared that the smoke would get into my lungs and give me problems again. I got out of sight, slumped to a curb, and waited for the weird feeling to hit. I waited and waited, but nothing happened. After ten minutes, I got up and continued my newspaper route. Annoyed with myself for being nervous over nothing, I threw a nice man's paper into a bush beneath his front picture window. Then I got an attack of guilt and fetched the paper out. And for being nice like that, I scraped my neck on a jagged branch.

Chapter Two

I sleep on my long-gone granddad Penrod's old bed frame. My dad gave it to me for my twelfth birthday. At the time, he said that it had a good, colorful history that I should be proud of. I never have been sure about the "proud" part, but I do believe it's got a colorful history. I sometimes tease Dad that General George Washington must have used it to block cannonballs during the Revolutionary War or that some rich guy threw himself and it out the window when he lost all of his money during the Great Depression. On top of being dented and chipped, it's notched and carved all over with a knife. It looks like an antique, all right.

For some reason, I used to play that Granddad Penrod's ghost spoke to me through his colorfully historic bed. I said that he kept me awake by disclosing his darkest secrets, which he had a few of on account of being a well-known womanizer. People all over town remembered him as a friendly, "flawed" person with a passion for the ladies, any and all of them. That's why saying he haunted my bed frame seemed funny, at least until the day I started hearing voices.

Hours after I scraped my neck, I was stirred from my dreams by rambling talk that wasn't my granddad Penrod and wouldn't have been comforting if it had been. Instead, I could hear my parents, who sleep downstairs. I covered my ears, but it didn't silence either one. My momma's voice kept harping about how my dad had gotten boring for her, boring and kind of fat, and that she was sick of hearing him complain about hard work. At the same time, my dad's voice said that he knew that the roofer who'd worked on our house had cheated him and that he wanted more pizza except his high cholesterol would take off.

I stayed quiet until I couldn't stand it, then, feeling idiotic, I begged them to keep personal issues to themselves. "Please. Just please," I mumbled, focusing on a poster I'd tacked to the slanted ceiling above Granddad Penrod's bed. In it, a man was stepping out a window and into thin air. The picture suddenly reminded me of how I felt, so I flipped around and examined the opposite wall. Then my bedroom door creaked open, and I realized I'd been talking loud enough to wake Matty.

"You okay, Penn?"

Trembling, I mumbled, "Matty?"

"What?"

"Are you hearing things?"

"Like what?"

"Voices? Momma's and Dad's."

He shook his head.

"I'm not either." I pulled the wool blankets around my small shoulders. Turning, I looked toward the window and into the purple Havre de Grace night sky, where the lights of a jet flashed like bits of a falling meteor over Millard Tydings Park and the big bay.

"Did you smoke another cigarette?" Matty asked, slipping around the door.

I shook my head.

Matty's expression, half-hidden by darkness, wrinkled sadly. At his feet, his shadow shot outward, touching the far wall and the iron coils of my radiator.

I tossed off my sheets and blankets and sat in my T-shirt and underwear trying to clear my head. I put my toes on the floor and closed my eyes and held my breath, wishing that my parents' voices would leave. They talked around each other, spun circles like ropes looping my brain, squeezing it tighter and tighter, giving me a terrible headache.

Seating himself beside me, Matty rested his hands on his knees and leaned against me. "It's gonna stop, Penn," he said. "It's gonna stop real soon, like the other time."

Late in the night, the voices finally did what he promised. But when they were gone, a heavy sadness, heavy like one of those library dictionaries, pressed against my chest, partially flattening me.

"Oh, God," I whispered. "I'm going crazy as hell. I can't believe it." I fell backward onto my pillow. Like hooks, tiredness grabbed at every piece and corner of my body, and I fell asleep.

In the morning, with the sky gray and overstuffed with dirty clouds, Momma shook me for almost five minutes before I woke. When I finally did, I felt the exact same way I had when, by mistake, I had gotten struck by a baseball in the eyebrow during P.E.

"Sweetheart," Momma said, leaning close and touching one of my cheeks, "are you sick?"

"No," I groaned. Even if I had to crawl, I planned on going to school. I wanted to put the voices behind me. I wanted the storm clouds in my brain to soar northward, and even if they wouldn't, I was going to act like they had.

Momma hovered over my bed as if she were going to say something, then she turned and clomped off to wake Matty.

As I stood up, my knees quivered pathetically, like there were tiny motors behind my kneecaps, shaking and shaking. I made my way to the bathroom. I dropped my clothes to the cold floor and turned the silver knobs in the shower so that water drummed against the tub. When steam started rising, I got in and stood beneath the spray. I moaned a few times, and just as my aching shoulders felt better, Matty banged in and sat with a thud on the closed toilet.

"Penn?"

"Yeah."

"You feel better?"

For a second, I considered acting like nothing had happened, except that I knew he'd tell my parents if I didn't instruct him not to. "I'm fine, Matty. I'm all right today, so don't worry. It's like nothing happened. I think I had one of those short fevers."

The smell of soap started making me nauseous. I washed quicker and let it rinse away down the drain. I shut off the shower. "Can I have some privacy?"

"You mean, you want me to leave?"

"Kind of."

I heard him get up and start for the door.

"Matty?"

"What?"

"Don't tell Momma or Dad about last night, okay? I'm fine. I feel real good right now."

After a pause, he said, "Okay."

As the door clicked closed, I rustled the flowery shower curtain back and struggled over the lip of the tub. I felt older than Granddad Penrod, except that I was still alive and he'd been gone a long time. I watched water drip from my body and land on the floor mat, leaving darker spots. I dried off and shuffled over to the sink. Wiping a clean place in the foggy bathroom mirror, I inspected my face and my chin with its three short, pale whiskers. I tilted my head sideways and stroked them, wishing more would sprout, that a thick, grassy beard would come in so that I might look like a lumberjack.

I examined the scrape on my neck. A dreary wave washed against me, and I swung the medicine cabinet door open and scooted things aside, grabbing a bottle of Bactine and squeezing it all over my scratch, hoping it would heal before school. In a certain type of light, I imagined it looked like a bad zit.

Shortly, dressed in my favorite pants and a pretty good T-shirt, I thumped downstairs. I entered the kitchen and tried to act relaxed, which was hard since I'd never needed to pretend to relax before.

Matty, who was sitting at the breakfast table eating a bowl of Cap'n Crunch and tinkering with a puzzle, glanced up and asked, "You wanna help me?" As he spoke, a piece of cereal fell from his mouth and stuck on his chin.

"No thanks."

Momma poured a cup of coffee. Her hair, the color of a tarnished nickel, gleamed softly in the kitchen light.

I asked if the scratch on my neck looked like acne.

"It doesn't. It looks like a scratch."

Nodding, working to look regular, I leaned my sore stomach against our old kitchen counter and ran my hands over the Formica.

"You sure you feel okay?"

"Yeah," I told her, forcing a grin. I tugged on my whiskers. "So, you think I oughta start shaving?"

"You can snip those with scissors."

"Momma, if I have to shave, I have to. I can't avoid it."

She smiled back. "Do you want me to get you a razor next time I go shopping?"

I nodded and waited a few moments before saying, "I was wondering, do you think Dad's getting sort of of fat?"

Momma laughed. "I guess I'm not the only one to notice?"

"You think?"

"He's gotten soft, is all, soft all over."

After a minute of feeling uncomfortable, I said, "I think I'm gonna have some cereal."

My momma and dad fell in love when they were still in high school. A few years younger, Momma watched Dad from a distance for months and months before, one night at the Burger King, she told him he looked sort of like Nick Nolte, this old actor. Back then, calling somebody Nick Nolte was a huge compliment. My dad was so pleased that just to impress Momma, he got into a fight. By punching it out with a black kid, he did impress her, too, because the guy broke my dad's nose, and even though it was crooked and bleeding, his eyes didn't water and he didn't even sniffle, not once. He says that the minute Momma talked to him, he was in love and wasn't about to look like a baby in front of her.

"Momma?" I said as I gulped down cereal.

"Yeah?"

"Does Dad complain a lot? Do you think he complains too much?"

She lowered her coffee cup and studied me seriously, which she's good at since she's a counselor at a family psychological clinic in town. "Penn, why are you asking me about your father?"

I lifted my shoulders. "I don't know."

She hesitated. "Well, my opinion on the matter is personal."

I didn't answer.

"He's got a touch of arthritis," she explained, which sounded like she was admitting that he did complain a lot. "It hurts him."

Matty added, "Sometimes he can hardly walk."

After eating, I set off for school. Usually I weave my way along streets and blocks without paying close attention to anything, but that morning, worried that I was heading for a long stay in a mental ward somewhere, was different.

Passing along Congress Avenue, I stopped and peered up the road toward Dr. Teeter's famous dental office. The crumbling house appeared soft and leaning. A glowing arrow sign hung from the collapsing front porch, pointing at the entrance. Far behind it, like a giant ship, the silver trusses of the Route 40 Bridge shined and nearly made me moan with sadness. As hopeless as Havre de Grace sometimes seemed, I didn't want to leave it for the nearest mental ward, which was probably in Baltimore. I liked the place all right. I liked its history, and the way the good and bad parts of mine fit into it.

Chapter Three

Dad says that way back in the 1930s, Havre de Grace was an important place. Mostly, migrating ducks made it that way. In the spring and fall, giant flocks filled the sky, a thousand dots combining together to make a single quivering mass of feathers. So many canvasbacks and mallards and geese rested on the headwaters of the Chesapeake Bay that one bad shot could hit five at a time. Hunters from everywhere took trains to town and stayed in fancy gingerbread hotels that have since gotten demolished. By the hundreds, folks filled Havre de Grace and blasted our birds and bought our famous hand-carved decoys.

And when they were tired of hunting, they wandered over to the race track, where glitzy gamblers from New York City bet on legendary horses—as legendary as a horse can get. It was something.

Between that sparkling time and this one, though, Havre de Grace yellowed and curled like old newspaper pages. People say it started when the duck and fish population was nearly ruined by commercial hunters and fisherman, and I suppose it slipped faster after World War II, when the race track lost what was left of its attractiveness and got shut down. For years, all locals could do was hope. They wanted something good to happen to our broken town, and hoping was all they could do. That's why I recognize that hope is almost as important as anything else.

But hope isn't reality. If you're drowning, you can't grab it like a life preserver. And, for sure, it won't come and fetch you like the Coast Guard. Unfortunately, after I'd heard voices a second time, it was all I had. I hoped and hoped that they would never return.

I kept a running tally of healthy days by doing what Granddad Penrod must've done when he was counting things: I scratched lines on his old bed frame. By the third ordinary day, I began to come up with excuses for what had happened. I wondered if the voices had been caused by a passing brain virus or maybe a weird bacteria

I'd gotten from a mosquito bite or an infected water fountain. I considered smog and cigarettes possible culprits. I even wondered about electricity, and if I was watching too much television or had the antenna on my radio facing toward my head too often.

A cold front accompanied by two days of tilting rain and rolling thunder barreled through. For the second or third time, our newly fixed roof leaked water into my bedroom, forming brown, amoeba patterns on my ceiling and filling buckets and pans every few hours. On my paper route, I had to wear a garbage bag for a raincoat since I'd lost mine. I knew I looked incredibly stupid, but that was okay with me. Everything was okay because the voices hadn't returned.

In the afternoons, while I delivered the *Havre de Grace Morning Document,* my mind slowly switched from considering my possible brain problem to Daisy. In fact, I began focusing my attention on her in order to occupy my thoughts with something good. I even devised a plan to get her notice. First I was going to start preparing for history class. Talking to Daisy was my aim, and I figured that to do it I needed to seem as smart and glad to learn as she did. So I began reading the textbook and every little photo description. Second, I figured that as soon as she noticed me, I'd talk to her. It wasn't a very intricate plan, but at least I had one.

The following Monday, when the class was invited to name things that Franklin Roosevelt did during the Great Depression, Daisy and I shot our hands up like opening railroad gates. When the teacher asked about the New Deal, we knew the answer. When he said Dust Bowl, I said there was a picture of a dust storm in our textbook. After just a couple of classes, I figured that Daisy couldn't avoid seeing our mutual genius for history.

On Thursday, we traded off answering more questions. Outside, it was a perfect fall morning, the kind my dad likes to go duck hunting on, nice fall days and dead ducks going hand in hand. Leaves helicoptered from trees that were beginning to look like gray pencil scratches in the sky, while golden sunlight streamed powerfully through our classroom windows, causing Daisy's skin and lips to glow, as if she were a famous singer in the spotlight.

My pulse bumped in my neck as if it were elbowing my throat for space. Then my enthusiasm drained away. As beautiful as Daisy was, attracting her was hopeless. Even if I learned everything in the textbook, she was too pretty for a short idiot like me. She'd never look extra-seriously into my eyes.

Discouraged, I sniffed hard at the air. I wanted to at least smell Daisy. During the two months I'd spent near her, I'd been trapped in the scent cloud from a girl who was closer by, and Daisy's smell, whatever it was, wasn't strong enough to creep through. That morning, not knowing her odor seemed tragic.

As I left class, my sneakers chattered on the floor. I went through Nineteenth-Century Literature wavering between miserable and angry even after the teacher put on a Civil War hat and jacket to discuss Stephen Crane and his skinny book, *The Red Badge of Courage*.

At lunch, the serving ladies scooped food into the various sections of a rectangular plate and handed it to me. I paid the cashier and wandered into the noisy dining room, where I stopped and studied my friends, who were all bunched up at our regular table. Hurlee had purchased or stolen himself a thick, gold necklace with a Mercedes medallion dangling from it, and everyone around him was admiring the thing like he owned the whole car instead of just a chopped-off piece. I shook my head. I didn't want to sit with them. I hesitated for a second before I turned and headed into a section of the enormous lunchroom I'd never explored in my year and a half at Havre de Grace High School.

Taking a seat, I glanced about, spotting a good number of students I'd known since the first grade. All of them belonged to different, separate groups that listened to specific music and shared different things they liked to do.

When I was done eating, I got up and, to my surprise, found myself walking a few steps behind Daisy, who was carrying her tray of dirty dishes toward the cleanup area, too. I tried not to act like I was doing it, but I studied her body, most especially her rear end. I smiled because she was wearing a purple sweater that kind of swayed slack around her little waist. As usual, she had on a pair of ironed pants that seemed as straight as a ruler. My heart pounded as we arrived at the dish corral. Daisy placed her dishes in the soapy pail and turned to leave.

"Sorry," I muttered, getting in her way as I bumbled about cleaning off my dishes. "My name's Penn. We've got history class together." I stuck my plate on top of hers.

She said, "You sit to my right."

"Me and you raise our hands a lot," I reminded her, just in case she didn't remember. "I guess we love history."

"I guess."

Worried that she might think I was boring, I tried to come up with a single riveting comment. "I've got a paper route in the afternoons."

Daisy smiled and stepped around me. Letting her pass, I stalked alongside so that the two of us weaved toward the dark school hallway. When we were halfway there, friends of mine called my name. I waved but

28

didn't answer. To Daisy, I said, "My older brother's retarded . . ." Then I ran smack into a black kid, nearly knocking the both of us to the floor. Apologizing, I caught back up to Daisy, then continued talking. "My older brother's retarded, and I'm not just saying that. He really is. But he's nice and sometimes doesn't seem that way. He can tell jokes, even. A lot of retarded kids can't do that."

Daisy nodded.

Stuffing my hands into my pockets, I searched my head for a question that would break our conversation wide open. My mind was paddling about when a genius idea came to me. "Hey, do you wish that Havre de Grace had a Chinatown? I sometimes do, even though I'm not Chinese. No one in my family is. But I like Chinese people and their food, especially fortune cookies. I also like the way Chinese people do stuff on television shows. They're real polite. You know, the way they bow and talk and all. Anyway, I guess Havre de Grace isn't big enough to have a Chinatown. Do you think? I mean, Baltimore doesn't even have one, and it's huge. Washington does, a little one. I've been there and seen ducks and chickens hanging in the restaurant windows. Do you like to eat chicken and duck? I do. I don't know about Wilmington or Philadelphia, but the most famous Chinatown is in San Francisco. It's the real well-known one, so I guess you wish you lived there sometimes, don't you?"

Daisy stopped and looked at me. She said, "I did live there, and if you think I'm Chinese, I'm not."

"You're not?"

"I'm Filipino. Filipinos and Chinese look totally different."

"They do?"

She nodded.

"Are Filipinos from Japan?"

"No."

"Oh." I itched the healing spot on my neck. "Everyone thinks you're Chinese."

"If they ever asked, I'd say I'm not."

"Nobody asks 'cause nobody's used to asking. Havre de Grace doesn't get many new people."

Daisy's gaze drifted off toward the faded red lockers around us. "I can tell."

"If you wanna tell people yourself, I could introduce you around so that everybody knows you're Filipino." My stomach felt like it was made of tin. "If you want, you could come with me on my paper route. I could introduce you around the whole town."

In a dainty, amazing way, her nostrils flared. "Maybe sometime."

"I know practically everybody and all sorts of things about Havre de Grace. I learned them from my momma and dad, who have good memories."

Daisy repeated, "Maybe sometime."

"I'm nice, you know. I'm not mean, and I wouldn't do anything stupid."

"I'll ask my parents."

I blinked. "That's good." Breathing in, for the first time I detected Daisy's scent, a perfect combination of strong underarm deodorant and perfume. It was better than any smell I'd ever noticed, better than makeup counters in department stores. It reminded me of wildflowers or tree blossoms from China, which I'd never smelled and where I couldn't stop thinking she was from.

Later that night, after dinner, Matty shuffled alongside me as I turned down blowy Lafayette Street. It was cold and dark out. The skies above were filled with scattered reddish clouds and the stars were as bright as string lights, even at seven in the evening. Wearing his winter coat, Matty looked stronger and more heroic than normal. Whenever his face came out of the shadows, he seemed like he was starring in a movie, like he was striking tough poses for the camera.

I told him about my day. "So anyway," I said, "her

name is Daisy, Daisy Parra, and she's not Chinese even though everyone thinks she is. Can you imagine?"

"Imagine what?"

"That she's not Chinese, but everyone thinks she is."

We stopped, and the wind bumped around Matty's sandy red hair. His expression got grim and serious, like he had to decide something that was more important than I could ever guess. "What's Chinese mean?"

"It means she's from China. It's a country," I explained, smiling at him. "It's across the Pacific Ocean. That's where I thought Daisy was from. Instead, it turns out she came from the Philippines, which I read this afternoon is a bunch of islands in the Pacific Ocean. Can you believe it?"

"No," he answered, sounding like he really was surprised.

We turned and headed along St. John Street, where lamps threw pretty patches across the dark cement sidewalks. We slowed in front of my personal favorite store, Totally Cowboy, which has display windows full of complex silver belt buckles and large, boot-cut blue jeans that flare like bullhorns at the ankle.

We got to the Canvasback Café, a coffee shop that also sells two flavors of ice cream and all sorts of desserts, and I held the door open for Matty.

Matty and I bought desserts and carried them to a

small table with a checkerboard pattern in the middle. Around us, familiar faces plowed through ice cream and cakes, their hands holding spoons the way people hold hammers. Matty buzz-sawed a couple of large cookies. Across from him, I ate a sundae and worked on a cola.

"Matty," I said, "you oughta meet a girl."

"Why?"

"So that you can do something other than work at Burger King. That's a sad way to live for a nice guy. It's a great big world out there." Not that I'd seen much of it. Ohio was the farthest west I'd ever gone, and Matty had been with me on account of there being a family wedding. I'd never been to New York City. For that matter, I'd never traveled farther north than Atlantic City, New Jersey. All together, I'd probably gone to Baltimore and Washington ten times in my whole life. As for girls and why they would make Matty's world seem bigger, I had no idea what I was talking about. Because I was feeling so good about Daisy and the like, I decided to give Matty untested advice. "Burger King isn't the end-all."

Matty swallowed. "I like Burger King enough."

I nodded. "Well, all I'm saying is that you should explore new things. I mean, you're older, you oughta try, you know, making it with a girl."

"Like kissing?"

"Yeah."

"I already have."

"Who've you ever kissed?"

"Somebody," Matty answered. "I'm not gonna tell." A tiny smile came onto his face.

I left my spoon dug into my ice cream and wiped my mouth. Edging a little closer to Matty, I narrowed my eyes, worried that the people around us would realize I hadn't ever kissed anything but my parents and the spot between our neighbor's cat's ears. "Did you really?"

"Yeah."

I tried to imagine who had possibly kissed him and wondered if it was one of the ladies at Burger King. "Was it nice?" I whispered, even though I knew it had to be. Every time I imagined smooching with a girl, I nearly detonated from strain, like a car that can't climb out of first gear.

"It was all right," he told me, his lips and cheeks coated with brown cookie crumbs.

I chopped at the sides of my sundae with my spoon, not quite as hungry as I had been. I found it annoying that my brother, with his little kid's brain, had kissed a girl before I had. It seemed wrong. On top of that, he hadn't even told me. I'd never known that he kept secrets, unless I told him to.

Matty's expression changed.

"What?" I asked.

He shook his head.

"Come on."

Matty lifted his hands helplessly. "Today, Momma said you're gonna be heading off to college soon. She told me at the grocery store."

"Yeah, so?"

"You'll be leaving."

"That's not for sure."

"She thinks it is."

I drew in my lips and bit on them. "It's a long time from now. I promise."

"Momma says it's soon."

"It's not."

Matty didn't seem convinced at all. He picked up a cookie crumb and put it in his mouth. After a minute, he said, "I'm glad you stopped smoking."

"It gave me a reaction," I said, and acted like it was a real tragedy. "Let's quit talking about annoying stuff, okay? Think of something good, like, what happened at work today?"

Matty smiled the way he does when he's explaining amazing topics. "Penn, there was a terrible thing. A girl forgot to put a hamburger in a man's bag, and he came back and said that she meant to do it that way. Then she got mad and . . ."

As he talked, I nodded, but I didn't listen so much.

Behind me, the coffee shop door banged open and shut loudly. I didn't even look. I was staring off, just being happy about Daisy, when a different voice hissed at me.

Surprised, I glanced around for who was talking, and my eyes flashed on Uncle Hewitt, who was making his way to the back of the coffee shop. At the old brass cash register, he ordered himself a cup of coffee.

Shivering and hearing odd sounds, I told Matty I wanted to go outside. Except, when I tried to rise, I was so screwed up that my arms and legs didn't want to work very well. Sweat beads formed on my skin so that the backs of my hands sheened beneath the old-fashioned ceiling lamps. A voice suddenly scolded me for not paying better attention to my brother's conversation. "I normally do," I promised.

Matty said, "What do you normally do?"

Scared, I mumbled some things that I didn't even understand.

"Huh?" Matty said, confused.

Uncle Hewitt staggered toward our table. He leaned near to me. After what seemed like a long time, he closed his lids. "Penrod, sweetheart?"

I finally stood. "Yeah?"

He ruffled back his lids. "Boy, tell me, is something happening you don't understand?" He flittered a hand in the air alongside one of his temples.

"Some, yeah."

He swallowed. "I . . . I can tell. And I understand it. Ya gotta know yer . . . yer not gonna be okay less ya get knowledgeable help and direction." His thin, wrinkled mouth flattened so that it seemed trapped behind the stubble hairs of his beard.

The voice suddenly said that it belonged to Uncle Hewitt. It told me my uncle controlled it and could make it stop. Terrified, I started moving backward away from him, my legs barely beneath me, sliding off in the wrong directions as if they weren't legs at all, as if they were empty pants with shoes threaded to the cuff.

Matty helped me get to the door and outside, into the Havre de Grace air. "You okay, Penn?" he kept asking.

Finally, I said, "Matty?" which didn't answer his question. I bent my neck and spotted the Canvasback Café's door. Framed in it was shrimpy Uncle Hewitt. He studied me as if I was a bug in a spider's terrarium, as if my life was about to get swallowed. His voice said, "You're not okay. You're not okay. You're not okay."

I begged Matty, "Let's go. Let's go home, please!"

Chapter Four

In Havre de Grace, few secrets stay that way. Most people know their neighbors' business. More than that, the town is small enough so that even if folks don't know somebody firsthand, they consider them neighbors. That's why, if you're a wild teenager with strict parents, you can sometimes have trouble getting away with things.

For example, the day after Uncle Hewitt struck fear into me, my dad stormed home from work with his brows angrily tilted and bundled like twigs on his bald head. He slammed the front door, took the stairs two at a time, his work boots throwing large hunks of dried mud, and marched into my room. That's how he caught me carving new marks on my bed, a groove to count my first normal day since an incident.

"What the hell are you doing, Penn?" he asked, breathing heavily. He unbuttoned the lower notches of his flannel shirt, revealing his greasy gray T-shirt beneath, the pouch of his gut, and a long, thin line of sweat.

Feeling separate from my body, I studied him from beneath Granddad Penrod's old bed frame. "I'm not doing anything," I answered, even though it was obvious I'd been carving.

"You're notching up your bed!"

"It's already carved on."

"Well, it doesn't need any more—that's for sure."

I slipped slowly out from under the side of the bed.

Dad crossed the creaky floor, leaned, and snatched the folding knife from out of my hands. "God, I'm pissed off at you," he said, flipping the blade closed and smashing the thing down on my old bureau.

"For marking the bed?"

"No," he shot back, "for getting drunk last night. For causing a scene at Canvasback's when me and your momma have warned the hell out of you about drinking."

Standing up, I gnawed at my fingernails and wished my dad wasn't angry and was instead interested in relieving my nerves. When he was feeling good, he had a nice, soothing personality and a good way of talking. He had a gift for saying nearly any rough thing from the bottom of his heart. It was his voice. It got heavy with strange love.

"You don't have a comment?" Dad asked, his brow crimped hard again.

"I wasn't drinking. You can ask Matty." I sat on the bed.

"Penn," he spouted in frustration, "you weren't drunk, but you couldn't hardly walk out of the shop? That doesn't exactly make sense, does it?"

"No, sir."

"Then you're lying to me. God, Penn, what has gotten into you?" he asked, his chubby face going limp, his hands grasping open and shut like he was still gripping bricks. "If you don't come around with a good answer, I'm gonna have to ground you. Either way, I'll tell you right now, I ain't gonna turn out a juvenile delinquent, not when I've worked hard to give you a good life and a fine, quality start. Do you appreciate what I'm telling you?"

"Yes, sir," I answered, knowing how sensitive he was to seeming low class, to how his relatives were mostly uneducated poor folk.

Like a whale's whisper, the sound of a train horn crept through my closed window. Somewhere nearby, a locomotive speared through the darkness. The sad moan repeated. Calmed by the familiar noise, my dad's sizable shoulders slowly unbunched like a crane cable going loose and dipping its shovel to the ground. With the backside of a wrist, he rubbed at the edge of his temple. Then he stepped over, rectangles and triangles of mud dropping from his thick soles, and seated himself close to me on the old bed. Taking some deep, relaxed breaths, he twisted about so that he was facing my profile.

"Penn, I ain't trying to make you do something I shouldn't have done. I mean, I drank beer when I was your age. I did, and I know you know that. I drink beer now. Thing is, I can do it 'cause I'm an adult. But I realize full well that I ain't got no good excuse for my former underage misbehavior except to say that I was wrong. When I was fourteen, my momma jumped ship and all I had left was my father. I guess that made me a little rowdy for a while." Rotating his gaze away, my dad peered into the hallway toward Matty's door. His bottom lip puffed outward a ways, and he appeared to be thinking on his life.

"Dad?"

He cleared his throat. "Like I was saying, I . . . I guess I was an unruly kid for a time, and I don't have a good excuse but to say I was troubled. But I truly believe we have given you a good, solid home life. For sure, you've had advantages over me when I was a kid. That's why I won't let you do what I did. I ain't gonna accept it. You understand where I'm going? I will come down on you hard and fast if you start that sorta thing."

"Yes, sir."

We were both quiet for a bit, my thoughts blank, like a box filled with air and darkness. Dad added, "And, Penn, just so you know, for your own information, right now your momma's in a low spot. She just is. She can't help thinking her life is a mess. That's the way she feels right now, and I can't hardly blame her. I mean, here she's gone and become a big successful social worker, and I'm complaining about arthritis, and Matty, he's retarded and won't ever not be. Do you get my point? We gotta be our best right now if we want your momma to feel her best. And if she knew you'd started drinking, she'd feel a whole lot worse. She'd think she's brought you up all wrong or that I carried bad genes into the mix or something. Nobody in their right mind wants to think that way. Do you see? This is about keeping your momma happy. That's why I'm asking you nice, right now, to stop misbehaving."

I told him, "I . . . would, Dad, except for I really wasn't drinking." My hands twisted and tied together on my lap. "It wasn't that. I promise."

Frustrated, elbows anchored solidly to his knees, my dad crashed his face into his hands. "Come on, Penn," he said in a terse, muffled voice. "I don't feel like including your momma in this mess, but I will. If need be, I will bring her in."

I pressed my eyes closed and didn't see any reason not to tell him the truth. I was weak-willed and over-cooked, and I couldn't hold on to that secret forever. "Dad, I wasn't drunk or drinking or anything. I swear. Here's the truth, if you wanna know it."

Air shot out of his nose and squeaked against his cal-loused palms. "Sure I do. If you ain't gonna feed me a load of bull, Penn, sure I'll hear you out. Go ahead."

I took a second before speaking. "The reason Matty helped me outta Canvasback's was because I was so scared of Uncle Hewitt that my legs wouldn't work the right way. They wouldn't get up under me. I suppose that's the reason I looked drunk to everybody. I would've thought I was drunk, too."

My dad lifted his face from out of his hands. "What the hell are you talking about? You were so scared your legs wouldn't work? What's that supposed to mean, Penn?"

My hands continued wheedling, desperate, in my lap. "It's the truth. It's what's been going on with me, things that don't make any sense. I've been hearing voices. I've been hearing them in my head, and Matty's seen it hap-pen. Like a week ago, in the middle of the night, I heard you and Momma talking, but you were asleep. I heard you guys as clear as day, and you were saying nasty things about each other and me and Matty, too."

My dad didn't speak.

"I'm hearing voices for some reason. They come in my head, but it's like they're coming through my ears."

Dad picked dried cement off his palm, rolled it between fingers, and threw it on the floor. "You're hearing voices?"

"Yes, sir. Last night was worse than ever, too, because they said it was caused by Uncle Hewitt."

"Who's they?"

"The voices."

"The voices said they were caused by Uncle Hewitt?"

"Yes, sir."

He took a few deep breaths. "You aren't bulling me?"

"No, sir."

Dad's eyes wandered. "Are you feeling sick or something?"

"No, sir, not sick. But I think . . . I think out of absolutely nowhere I might be going crazy or something. I'm scared I might be. That's why I was carving on the bed. I keep a record of how long it's been between when voices come."

My dad rubbed a hand across his cheeks and mouth. "Penn, sweetie, I'm not exactly sure, but I think this might be a real type of problem. Normal people don't hear voices is all, not if they aren't sick-feeling."

"I know," I answered, getting a little more worried.

"God Almighty," Dad said. Ignoring my long-standing instructions not to give me a hug, he leaned over and slapped his arms around me and jostled me in a loving way, in the way he can. He jammed his nose against my head, mooshing his nostrils so that I could feel his wet breath against the roots of my hair.

"Sorry," I told him, feeling guilty.

"It ain't your fault, sweetie."

"I don't think it is."

We sat quiet for a few minutes. As his breath tranquilized me, as the room got darker, he let go. Slowly, his sad look changed, and he put a hand under my chin. "You know what? I take it back. I bet this all goes away. I bet you're gonna be okay. I can feel it inside, like woman's intuition, except for, you know, I'm a man. You're a good, normal teenage boy, and you're gonna be fine. This is just a momentary problem that's gonna disappear. Maybe it's just hormones. Maybe it's a flu. Who knows, but it ain't permanent."

"You think?"

"Oh, yeah. Craziness just doesn't happen to a boy who's been normal his whole life. It doesn't hit sudden like that."

"Really?" I asked, worried he had no idea what he was talking about.

"Oh, yeah, really." He sat silent for a while. "I ain't even gonna tell your momma about this. I don't think she needs to be troubled by something that's gonna disappear as fast as it comes. We'll just let it pass, and when she feels better, me and you are gonna tell her and laugh about it."

"All right," I agreed, seeing his point despite the fact that Momma, when it comes to people going crazy, knows more than him.

Dad kissed my temple and gave me another squash. In due course, he said, "I'm sorry I accused you of drinking."

"Sorry about scratching up the bed."

He snorted. "Go on and carve your chart if it makes you feel better. My daddy's bed already looks like a totem pole." Smiling nice, he winced and grunted and stood painfully. With the toe of his boots, he tried to scatter away the squares and triangles of mud from off his treads. "Your momma hates when I track dirt inside."

"I'll brush it out of sight."

He scratched his scalp. "Thanks." He gave me a good inspection. "You gotta keep me informed about the voices. Really. It's important even though I know it's nothing. Okay?"

"I will."

"But you can't worry so much, either. That'll just make it linger. Worry makes things linger, is what your momma tells me."

My dad's confidence got me feeling better. Over the weekend, I was voice-free, so that by Monday, I was pretty optimistic and thinking that the dark clouds of insanity had changed directions, like a storm over the Susquehanna.

At school, spilling over with relief and hope, I decided to start eating lunch alongside Daisy in the cafeteria. Granddad Penrod had been famously assertive and successful with women, so I figured I might be able to get away with being forward on account of sharing the same magnetic blood. Plus, I knew that she sat and ate alone and might be lonely.

That entire school week, I located myself in front of Daisy, and not once did we discuss history or scholarly topics. Instead, I made her laugh by telling her little things about Havre de Grace and the way Matty stops in the middle of stories, making it hard to figure what he means. I said that our history teacher's nervous upper-lip twitch sometimes makes him look like a growling dog, and, even though he's a real nice guy, we both went hysterical over that. Another time, she complained that the

Havre de Grace humidity made her hair frizzy, leading to a conversation about how California has such dry air that everyone's hair stays flat and you barely ever sweat, even in the summer.

At home, I read as much about the Philippines as I could find. I wanted to impress Daisy with the way I respected her country and how she wasn't completely American. As a matter of fact, the following Saturday, as a soft snow fell, me and Matty walked up to the Havre de Grace Public Library so that I could research more on the Philippines while he looked through sports magazines.

"Hey, Penn?"

"Hey what?"

Matty looked up from a *Sports Illustrated*. "Who's your favorite basketball player?"

"That tall skinny guy."

"Which one?"

"I don't know his name, but he wears a knee brace."

"Yeah," Matty said softly, like he knew who I meant. "I always wish I was good enough to play in the NBA."

"I wish you were, too," I told him. And I really did. He deserved something like that after the bad luck that had started his life.

When we were finished, we wandered over to Washington Street and got ourselves a bag of doughnuts and two hot chocolates. We went south to the Concord

Point Lighthouse and wandered to the end of the public pier. Turning, the two of us looked toward the widespread mouth of the Susquehanna River. Within minutes, a train streaked past on a girder bridge, making the area so pretty it didn't seem possible we were still in Havre de Grace. I smiled because I liked our town, and after a week of being healthy, I felt healed. Maybe my dad had been right about mental illness not striking so unexpectedly. Under Granddad Penrod's old bed, I was still keeping a tally of days since the incident at the Canvasback Café, but I considered quitting.

The following Monday, I went to lunch, excited to discuss the Philippines with Daisy but wanting to be subtle about it. By the middle of the week, though, I was tired of being subtle. Real pleasantly, as if I always talked about international news, I asked Daisy about the wife of Ferdinand Marcos, the former dictator. "Did you know that Imelda Marcos had one of the biggest shoe collections ever?"

"I did," Daisy said, smiling. "Mom and Dad told me."

"Oh." I took a bite of my lunch. "Did you know that Mount Pinatubo, that volcano that exploded a while ago, had been dormant for six hundred years? Can you believe it? Out of nowhere, it just stopped being dormant."

"Did it?" she said, grinning at me like I wasn't too bright.

"Yeah. Out of nowhere," I told her, wiping the tips of my fingers on a napkin. "My favorite thing about the Philippines is that they've got rubber trees. Can you imagine how cool those are?" Pausing, I asked, "What's your favorite thing?"

She sipped her milk. "I don't know."

"You don't?"

"I've never been to the Philippines."

I slid way down in my chair. "You've never been?"

"Never."

"Well, you should go," I said, scooting back up. "It's where you're from. You oughta see what your country is like."

She shrugged. "Penn, where's your family from?"

"They've practically always been around here."

"Yeah, well guess what?"

"What?"

"I was born in Texas, and I feel pretty American. I like American music. I like American movies. I like American books. So even though I look Filipino, I don't feel like the Philippines are where I'm from. You know what I mean? I feel American."

My cheeks got hot. "I didn't mean it that way."

"I know."

I sat quiet. "But being Filipino is what makes you pretty. I mean, you're real pretty in a Chinese sort of way. And you move nice."

Daisy's dark face turned pink.

I told her, "You're the best-looking girl in all of Havre de Grace. That's the truth."

She laughed. "Stop, okay?"

"It's true," I declared, as if she could read about it in the *Havre de Grace Morning Document*.

"Don't," she said, so that I realized she really did want me to quit saying nice things, which was weird since I wished like hell she'd say them to me.

I leaned forward. "If you ever wanna learn about the Philippines, just ask me. I've been reading about them. Okay? Just ask me, 'cause I was trying to impress you even though I did it the wrong way. That's why I know all about the different islands and what they make and the fact that they've got water buffalos and mongooses."

Daisy looked at me and said, "Penn, you impress me. You don't have to study the Philippines."

"I don't?"

"You impress me enough," she repeated, which sounded both good and bad.

"So, you . . . you wanna come on my paper route this afternoon?"

She placed the ball of her napkin down, and it

started to open, slowly, like a flower. "I can't. I forgot to ask my mom."

"Will you, for tomorrow, maybe?"

"Maybe," she answered, and with that word, the cafeteria, with its high ceiling rafters and spindly columns, exploded inside me like a cup of ignited gasoline. Till the bell rang, it was my favorite room in town, nicer even than the foyers of those fancy bed and breakfast hotels along Union Avenue, where they don't allow dust balls or bad language of any sort. For a few minutes, the lunchroom felt like paradise.

Chapter Five

The next day, before history, I waited by the door to say hello to Daisy. When I saw her coming, I smiled.

"You're making me nervous," she joked.

I said, "Sorry," and changed the way my smile went.

When class was done, I waited by the door again, where she said, "See you at lunch?" before fading into a lacework of shoulders and elbows.

In Nineteenth-Century Literature, we discussed *Billy Budd,* by Herman Melville, which is a boring-as-hell book about a sailor who's such a good person he's like Jesus. I could hardly stand listening to the discussion, so I drew on my desk. Our teacher, who was wearing a nineteenth-century sailor suit and carrying a canoe paddle, scuffed around barefoot talking about the guy. "Billy this" and "Billy that." No matter how "historically dramatic" he got—which is a term he liked to use—I wasn't interested in a guy who was so nice everybody thought he was perfect.

At lunchtime, I dumped my books and made for the cafeteria, got my tray loaded, and marched between people and over to Daisy, who regularly arrived before me. I arranged myself across from her and blurted, "So, did you find out if you can go on my paper route?"

She wavered. "Well . . . my mom says as long as I'm home before my father, it's fine."

I smiled so wide my lips hurt. "What time's that?"

"Around five," she estimated, bobbing her head slightly, so that her black hair swayed about her ears. "What're you planning to show me?"

My grin faded. I shifted and picked at a slice of bread. "Nothing really, just town and all that. Things on my paper route." I made a funny face. "Why?"

"Because I might bring a notepad to write details down."

"Really?"

"Yeah."

I tried to appear open to the strange idea. "So, where do you live?"

"Just a short walk from here." Daisy tilted against the table and surprised me by lifting one of her hands and placing it on the back side of one of mine. Excited, I wondered if maybe she had started thinking of me like a boyfriend. I glanced down at her hand and admired how her fingers were nice and dry instead of clammy, like mine. Then Hurlee and his friend Burris sat down on either side of me, so that I was stuck between them.

Daisy yanked her hand away.

"Yo, cuz," Hurlee said.

"Yo," I said back.

"This who ya been hanging with?" Hurlee jerked a shoulder in Daisy's general direction.

"I've been meaning to tell you guys, but I keep forgetting."

"Must be love."

Daisy blushed, and I could feel the heat rise in my face.

Hurlee licked his lips and itched at the base of his neck, just below his curly hair that resembled a tan tumbleweed with a root ball stuck to it. He looked at Daisy. "Yo, ya bring my boy back by our table some, huh?"

"I will," she said softly, but I knew she wouldn't fit in over there.

Hurlee picked between his teeth with a finger and

swiveled back to me. He held up the Mercedes medallion he'd been wearing around school. "What'cha think, homey?"

"Did you cut it off a car?"

"Witta hacksaw."

"It's nice."

Burris said, "We looking for another Mercedes, 'cept it don't seem like there's one in town." He reached down and tore at the hole in his blue jeans. Besides being about six-and-a-half feet tall, he had acne craters that made his long, stretched face seem molded from wax that'd been struck by a shower of searing pebbles. I always felt sorry for how he looked and wondered if something could be done to fix his skin.

Hurlee stood and leaned toward Daisy. "Yo, name's Hurlee."

"I'm Daisy."

"Nice to meet ya, Daisy."

She smiled shyly.

Hurlee rotated his wild, naturally dilated eyes back onto me. "Cuz, ya want, we gonna be at the Citgo after school. Ya stop by and I ain't gonna tease ya none about not smoking or nothing."

"You can tease me."

"Thought I might've made you mad."

"You didn't." I got up, and we thumped fists and banged shoulders like always, then Hurlee and Burris said, "Later," and left through the crowd.

I turned, and it was obvious Daisy was bothered by something about their visit. I wondered if she didn't like how low down they seemed.

"Hurlee's my cousin. Burris is a friend of his." I sat and rested my arms on the edge of the table. "They're not the smartest people in the world, but they're nice."

She said, "Must be cool to have a cousin in town."

When the last bell of the day clanged, I snatched a few things from my locker and went out Havre de Grace High School's graffiti-covered metal doors. At the corner of Adams Street, away from the crowds, I stopped and waited for Daisy by studying the sky, which was filled with flat, flat greenish clouds that reminded me of a world map, as if I was standing on the moon and peering back at Earth.

"Hey," I said when she walked up.

"Hey."

I didn't know what else to talk about and stood there in near panic before managing, "You hear that train horn?"

She nodded.

"It's either Amtrak or a freight train. It's probably going to New York City, which is where I always wanted to go because some of my family lives up there."

"You'll go."

I felt like I was standing on the moon again, and asked, "You wanna hear something about town?"

"Why not?"

I thought for a second. "I bet you didn't know we had a race track. We were a little famous for that. When my uncles and granddads weren't working other jobs, a few of them worked there. They took bets. One of them was fired for stealing money, even."

"That's terrible."

I laughed because, around town, those types of stories were common. Guardedly, I told her, "I . . . I always visit my brother before I go on my paper route. It's my routine. Do you mind? He's at the Burger King."

She removed her thick glasses and wiped the lenses clean on a part of her jacket. She fixed them back on her nose and ears. "I'd like to meet him."

Shortly, we were standing in line behind students and soldiers from the Aberdeen Proving Grounds. Near the counter, I called, "Hey, Matty! This is Daisy."

"Hey, Daisy," he answered back, not looking retarded at all.

"Hey," she said.

Afterward, we sipped our sodas and walked slowly toward the *Havre de Grace Morning Document* offices. Not knowing exactly what to discuss, I showed Daisy important locations in town, like the curb I rode my bike off when I was little, banging my chin against the handlebars. "It hurt," I explained. "My momma said that for a kid my size, it was like going over Niagara Falls."

"It's a big drop."

Next, I told her, "That corner is famous for a guy who disturbed the peace during the Depression. He was drunk and out of work, yelling cusswords up at a priest who couldn't stand bad language. That priest had a terrible temper and shot the guy from out of a rectory window with his duck gun."

Daisy held the straw of her soda against her teeth. "Did he die?"

"He lost a hand. After that, he had a hook, like a pirate. He worked on the water, and when they let out nets to catch fish, he had to be careful not to get it caught on a rope."

At the newspaper office, I introduced Daisy to Rhonda, the secretary, then I dragged my stack of *Havre de Grace Morning Document*s outside.

"This area of town isn't so nice anymore," I told her as I rolled newspapers. "But it used to be nice. It used to be busy all the time. I mean, every building was filled with a store. That's before I was born."

She regarded the shabby storefronts and squadrons of pigeons that had built their nests in and on them. A few people walked past.

"It's ugly. I already know it is," I admitted, stuffing my newspaper sack full. "But it could be nice."

"You could write a lot of sad poems in a place like this. Somebody probably has."

"I bet nobody has." I stopped and looked up. "Do you write stuff or something?"

She shook her head. "Sometimes. Mostly poetry. My own personal hero is Maya Angelou. Do you know who she is?"

"No. I mean, I'm not excited about poetry since I can't rhyme very well."

Daisy raised her pretty eyebrows. "Poetry isn't about rhyming."

I shrugged and adjusted the strap of my newspaper bag. "I thought it was. You ready?"

She nodded.

"So," I told her at the end of the block, "now I'm gonna show you how nice Havre de Grace is. Right off, we're gonna go by a part of Union Avenue where a guy ran over a fox and got it stuffed for his mantle."

Daisy frowned. "That's not nice—that's disgusting."

I smiled and started to tell all types of stories about the various big events that had occurred in Havre de

Grace, like how it had gotten burned by the British during the War of 1812. Along the way, I avoided the shutdown Citgo gas station for fear it would be awkward introducing Daisy to so many friends at one time. Anyway, it already seemed like the afternoon was moving too fast, and I didn't want to waste more of it.

Finally, before five, we headed for her home, which was on the south side of town, not so far from where I lived. Drifting down past my house, we hung a right on Commerce Street, edging Millard Tydings Park, where Matty and I sometimes fished. Then we turned and looped down Chesapeake Drive, arriving at the gates of Havre de Grace's only luxury condominium complex, The Water's Edge.

"This is it," she said.

I laughed. "Not really?"

She laughed back, "It is."

The fancy brass plates on the gate flashed in the headlights of an expensive car. I explained, "Mostly army officers live here."

"That's what my dad is."

"Oh," I mumbled, and scratched my head, before suddenly worrying that she might think I had lice.

Daisy took off her book bag and dug around in it looking for something. Stepping close, she put a piece of paper in my hand. "It's my phone number."

We looked eye-to-eye.

I said, "Okay."

She leaned and kissed me with her spongy lips, so that I could taste her makeup and perfume together. "Thanks for the afternoon, Penn," she said as I hyperventilated. "I had fun."

"Me too."

"Maybe you can call me tonight?"

"I can."

When she'd disappeared through the gate, I waited a second before heading down the roadway. I was so excited that instead of going straight home, I walked the edge of Millard Tydings Park. Slouching onto a bench, I looked out over the grass and beyond the trees at a narrow patch of swamp filled with skinny, swaying grasses and behind those, the broad Chesapeake Bay. My childhood life seemed to be teetering at the edge of my adulthood, and that was thrilling. I liked how I was getting older and expanding my wings, becoming less like the kids I grew up with and more like someone I'd never known.

Chapter Six

The following afternoon, as I stood examining my stack of newspapers in the yellowy light of the *Havre de Grace Morning Document* offices, Rhonda declared that she was itching to get home to her young daughter, who was stuck in daycare on account of her husband's income being insufficient and her having to work. She always talked about that stuff, so I listened quietly, like usual. Really, it was a sad situation made worse because, to Rhonda's way of thinking, they could've gone without two cars, cable television, and cell phones. If they did, at least she could've been a part-time momma. The problem was that her husband didn't feel any of that stuff was extravagant, and that made Rhonda hellaciously mad at him.

Turning, I answered, "Yeah, that's weird he won't sacrifice. My parents did. My momma and dad didn't have me till Matty went into first grade. They said they waited because they couldn't afford two daycare payments. But they never had cable television, and they still don't have cell phones, so I know it's true."

Rhonda lowered her pink cat's-eye glasses. "What?"

Straightening, I told her, "I agree that those things are extravagant. That's all."

"Penn, honey, what are you talking about?"

"Your husband and how he thinks extravagant things are necessary instead of extra."

"Was I talking out loud?"

"Yeah," I told her, and dragged my paper bundle through the door and onto the sidewalk.

Outside, with the door closed behind me, Rhonda kept talking, clear as day. She said that it was comical how she didn't realize she'd been yammering out loud.

I looked in through the glass and saw her answer the phone. Nervous, I started untying the string around my papers, and, just as it was coming loose, another person entered my head. I looked up to make sure someone wasn't actually talking to me, and there was Kenney, one of the owners of the Canvasback Café.

My round eyes caused him to stop.

"What?" Kenney asked.

"Nothing."

"You sure?"

"Yes, sir."

"You look like you want to say something."

"I don't."

He brushed a hand across his cheek, and I heard him, or a voice like his, consider the weird way I was acting and remember how, the week before, I had made a scene in his café. Suddenly, his voice asked if I was behaving strange because I wanted to confess gayness.

Irritated, I said, "I'm not gay."

Kenney didn't answer.

"I don't wanna talk about it," I told him, turning my back.

He lingered—on account of being frightened for my mental state, I think.

"Please," I begged him over a shoulder.

Nice as he was, he abided and started walking. However, after going about twenty steps, he pivoted and called, "You sure?"

I waved and got out a bag of rubber bands. Slowly,

like the volume on a radio that was getting turned up, new voices began playing around Kenney's and Rhonda's. They said that the name of the newspaper ought to change to fit the afternoon delivery schedule and that Havre de Grace should be abandoned to pigeons. I shook my head hard, which seemed to cause a flood of different conversations, as if shouts and whispers were bouncing down the street.

Scared, I left my newspaper pile where it was and lurched across the street. I tried to escape around a building and along the ruins of a Green Street warehouse. As if I was wearing seventy-pound shoes, I lurched through a patchy, littered field where a canning factory had been, eventually arriving at the old wooden bulkhead surrounding Havre de Grace. The strong tar smells of the pilings cleared my thoughts, and, for a moment, the voices faded.

Breathing hard, I stared out at the water and the white porcelain boats and a red tug with seagulls following behind, twirling like flower petals in a lottery ball machine. The voices suddenly returned, and I collapsed into a patch of tall, hard weeds and broken glass, where I curled tight and began hiccupping and crying because I knew I was going to get locked in a padded cell. I knew I'd gone and lost my mind.

Hours passed, and the conversations rose and fell. Trains moved across the black railroad bridges, heading both north and south. The sky grew dark and my side thumped painfully. Some kind of sharp object was stabbing into it. I didn't care if blood dumped out of me by the gallon. Being that I was an indescribable lunatic, dying in a patch of weeds seemed appropriate and even merciful.

It wasn't till late that I was finally left alone, and I dragged myself from off the ground. Standing painfully, bottle caps and rocks falling from my clothes, I narrowed my eyes to the clear, frosty sky and the layers and layers of white stars. It was absolutely beautiful, a perfect picture. Swallowing, I started weakly across the blue-tinged field toward the dying shopping district. Steam curled from my nostrils and my hands were practically numb. At the *Havre de Grace Morning Document* offices, my stack of papers was gone from the sidewalk. In case it had rolled away, I looked around and between buildings, but it wasn't there. Trembling, I headed for home.

Staggering along, I felt like a ghost, like I was halfway real and halfway somewhere else. Near the hospital, on Union Street, cars shooshed slowly past until one set of headlights lit against my shoulders and didn't go by.

Behind me, my dad pulled over and jumped out of his pickup. "Penn!" he shouted, rushing around the hood. He turned me to look at him. "Penn, sweetie?" he said, his voice scratchy.

"Dad?"

"Where the hell have you been?"

It took a second for me to answer, to figure out what to say. "The voices came back."

He dabbed his nose and struggled with his words. "When?"

"This afternoon."

My father nodded and hugged me. "Don't . . . don't you worry at all. It's okay. It's gonna be okay."

Lifting a cold thumb, I pointed toward downtown. "I gotta go back and find my newspapers."

"They ain't there. I delivered 'em. Rhonda called the house and said you abandoned your pile, so I went down and did the delivery."

I stared at the toes of my shoes. "That's good."

He hesitated before saying, "Penn, we gotta get you some help, sweetie. It's probably not anything too bad, but we gotta get you help."

"Yeah."

"We gotta tell your momma about the voices."

"I figured."

"Tomorrow," he said. "We'll tell her tomorrow. She had a bad day, and she's angry at you."

When I came into the kitchen, Momma didn't hide how pissed off she was for how I didn't come home for dinner, for scaring her.

"Sorry," I told her.

"Sorry doesn't cut it," she informed me, glaring.

"Sorry," I said again, not knowing what would cut it. I lifted an arm and winced at the pain in my side.

Momma leaned down, turned me gently, and fear suddenly gripped her face. My backside was gummed up with blood. "Oh, my God!" Momma cried.

Dad sputtered, "I didn't see that."

"Penn," she said, "what did you do?"

"Just stumbled onto some glass. I fell."

"Truly!" She stripped off my coat, then hung it on a chair and gently untucked my damp shirt, rolling the fabric up to my armpit. With a wet paper towel, she wiped away the dried blood.

My dad leaned down. "It's nothing. See, Belinda?"

"Well, it sure bled a lot."

"Does it hurt?" Matty wanted to know.

"Naw," I said, and it really didn't.

He scratched his chin. "Looks like you were stabbed a lot of little times."

"I wasn't."

"Looks like it."

Momma said, "I don't think you need stitches, but it doesn't look great."

Dad told me, "I've had worse."

Momma lowered my messy shirt and frowned. Standing, she mopped her hands on a dishtowel and made a suggestion. "Penn, go take a hot shower and wash that off with some soap. Really scrub it. I'll deal with you tomorrow."

That night, black-ink exhaustion froze my body. I fell asleep with my arms folded across my chest like a dead Egyptian pharaoh. Six hours later, before anyone roused me, I popped awake in the same weird position. Rising from the sheets, I felt completely sad about the early end to my pretty fun life. I wondered where Momma, who had a list of hospitals for people suffering from mental illnesses, would want to send me when Dad told her about my problem.

I went into the bathroom, tugged down my undershorts, and rested atop the toilet. Elbows on my knees, I stared at the slightly wavering shower curtain and wondered exactly which mental illness I was getting. I wasn't familiar with the different types, but I knew there was a whole slew to pick from. Momma, who wasn't even a doctor, had about fifty books on the subject, some of them bigger than briefcases.

What worried me was getting treated like my fifth-grade science teacher, who had seemed normal until he started wrapping rolls of barbwire around his chest and wrists. Even after that, he was friendly, until going off to a mental hospital. When he came back from that place, he could hardly even say his name, much less act nice. For that reason, I used to wonder if they had ruined the good part of his brain when they were trying to repair the bad. The only positive thing that occurred after he was hospitalized was that he stopped wearing barbwire clothes, something that must've hurt.

I swallowed and looked at my white feet. I wiggled my toes and watched them cast tiny, moving shadows across the dusty tiles and lines of grout. I wasn't sure when my dad was going to spill the news, but I kind of hoped he was planning to do it after work. Even though I was crazy, I wanted to sit with Daisy at lunch, figuring it might be my last chance. Certain types of unhinged people are cool to be seen with, but being friendly with a truly insane person would likely demolish her reputation so that she wouldn't want to be caught talking to me.

After showering, I went back to my room and chose

my clothes. Hair brushed, I went downstairs and found my dad waiting for me in the foyer. He said, "We've got to talk," and led me into the living room. "I told your mother," he said.

I nodded.

"Let me go get her."

When Momma came in, I could tell she'd been bawling, which I hated. "Momma," I told her, "you don't have to worry. I'm healthy now."

"Penn," she answered, biting at the knuckle of a finger.

"What?"

"Voices don't just start and then suddenly stop for good."

I played upbeat. "But they have. I can tell. Last night was it."

She wiped at her cheeks and said, "Dear, what you've got sounds like something I'm familiar with. It sounds like it could be something I know about."

I tried to appear bored.

"It's called schizophrenia." She hiccupped. "Its onset frequently comes during adolescence. Penn, it is a very serious mental illness, one in which people can experience a range of symptoms, like hearing voices or hallucinating. It needs to be treated with medication. It has to be."

"That's not my problem," I told her matter-of-factly. "I had a parasite or something that's finally gone."

Dad rubbed his arthritic hands together, wincing. He sat in a chair and picked mud hunks the size of dimes from off the tops of his boots. "Penn, your momma's a professional mental healthcare worker. She knows what she's saying. This could be a serious situation. Okay?"

"But it's not."

"It could be," Momma declared. "But . . . we need to get you examined."

I turned my head. I wanted my life to continue the way it was.

Momma said, "We can't ignore this, Penn. We can't. You need medical attention."

Glancing at the television, I imagined myself watching an early morning cartoon, laughing. I'd never known how lucky I was to be regular. "Can we wait till Monday, please?"

"We shouldn't."

"Please. Just till Monday."

"Why?"

I stared at her. "For things going on at school."

Momma swayed back and forth and touched sadly at the sleeve of my shirt. She paused, tears streaking her face, before saying, "You tell me. Can you wait?"

"Yes."

"Penn, voices just don't show up."

I tried to look calm. "But you won't do anything till Monday?"

"I'll wish them away. I'll beg. I'll make a deal with God. And I'll respect your wishes."

Chapter Seven

On Friday, I slapped on my backpack and zipped up my coat. I told my mother I was fine, then I shot out and along the sidewalk. I went up two blocks to Lafayette Street, hoping to catch Daisy on her way to class. Hustling along, I noticed the crackle of dry leaves in bushes and songbirds chirping. I felt pretty good even after my mom had called me sick.

On the roadway, cars hummed by innocently, the bright morning light gleaming on their sharp edges and along the boundaries of deep dents. It was freezing and only a week from Thanksgiving, but I felt the way I do in the spring, when the winter's been long and the sun's finally shining and warm. I wanted to sit in the grass and enjoy the warmth, any warmth.

Daisy wasn't anywhere to be found, so I went on to school, where the rooms glowed wonderfully, their walls perfectly painted. Checking my watch, I hurried down to Daisy's locker. She wasn't there. I waited a bit, but she didn't show up. I tried to sneak a look through one of the vents in the metal door, but it was too dark to see anything. I waited a little longer, then headed off to fetch my books.

Climbing the skinny stairwell to the second floor, I glanced out a large window overlooking the street, at a garbage can that crows were working over. They jumped gracefully from rim to rim as if they were filled with helium. Each took turns pecking at a white fast-food bag, tossing pieces to the wind. Then I was carried along by the pushing crowd.

As I opened my locker, a note fell out. I picked it up, unfolded it, and read:

Hey, Penn, maybe I can help you
with your papers this afternoon?
Daisy

I stared at the note like it was a photograph of her face. Curious, I even sniffed it. Daisy's smell wasn't there, which was okay since, overall, her writing looked exactly like I'd hoped it would. Each letter was sophisticatedly tilted and flowed cleanly into the next. Her penmanship seemed mature and womanly, not like a girl, especially the girls I'd grown up with.

Carefully tucking the note between the fraying walls of my wallet, I felt an unexpected rush of joy. It seemed impossible, but I finally had a girlfriend, and she was smart and beautiful and laughed a lot.

I got to algebra before the bell rang. Taking out my pencil, I started drawing when my math teacher, Ms. Lang, who's impossibly short and wears a wrist brace, said how tired she was and that, sometimes, all the money in the world didn't seem like enough pay for her job. She was sure she had burnout from teaching kids who didn't want to learn, from seeing the same class-room every day, and eating lunch in the teachers' lounge.

Sure that her confessions were leading to a giant classroom reprimand, I kept my head down. I wasn't horrible at algebra, but it wasn't a subject I enjoyed. Mostly, I didn't want to get a speech about laziness. I got them a lot and hated the ones Ms. Lang gave most of all.

The girl beside me piped up and told Ms. Lang that, in case she didn't know, she was absolutely disgusting. She said Ms. Lang was pale and flabby and annoyed all the time. Plus, there were days when Ms. Lang smelled bad, so that nobody wanted to breathe around her.

I laughed and thought that Ms. Lang was going to send the girl to the principal's office, but she didn't.

Then a kid behind me began discussing a computer game. Alongside him, another girl mentioned her painted fingernails and wondered if the color was right.

Curious, I glanced back toward where her hands should've been, only to find that she hadn't arrived yet. I frowned and looked about at all my classmates, who appeared to be waiting silently for the bell to sound. Up by the blackboard, Ms. Lang's voice asked what would happen if she faked a collapse during the middle of class. The real Ms. Lang didn't say anything.

The bell clanged, hurting my head. Noises filled my misfiring brain and spontaneously straightened my legs so that I stood up from my desk like a cigar store Indian.

Ms. Lang pointed a piece of chalk at me and told me to sit. Without using her mouth, she said that she was sick of trying to teach kids like me, idiots and thugs with no potential.

"But I've got potential," I protested.

"What?"

"I'm not a complete thug."

Furious, she spouted, "Penrod, take your seat!"

A boy who lived down the block from me said I was a moron, so I turned and told the class, "Algebra's not my favorite subject, but I'm not stupid. I'm—" Sweat began rolling down my back, and my shirt sucked flat to my skin. Simultaneously, my eyesight darkened a few notches.

Ms. Lang informed me that I was ruining her lesson plan. Grabbing her grade book, she threatened me with a poor mark.

"God," I replied, "don't you think I might be sick? Don't you think I might not mean to be acting this way?"

"Sit!" Ms. Lang screamed.

Voices whispered that I was a troublemaker, so I defended myself. "Actually, I'm not a troublemaker, and I never was. It's just my cousin Hurlee, who likes to have fun. He . . ." Unable to think clearly, I paused. Hundreds of different people seemed to be bouncing about inside my brain. I felt like a lightning rod in a hurricane. Scared, I heaved forward, crashing into desks. Catching myself, I straightened and tried to tell people not to worry, that I was fine except for having a small bout of schizophrenia. Then I staggered sidelong, as if I'd been pushed. I crashed through more rows, twisted, and fell, cracking my skull against the shiny tile floor. A black smoky world surrounded me, and the storm that I'd tried to ignore for weeks swept in.

I don't like to be sick. I don't like to feel weak and needy. I don't like being in bed with wrinkly clothes on, and I don't like it when people have to fetch me things. I despise those feelings. Unfortunately, when I got back from the Havre de Grace Hospital's emergency room, a concussion rattling my low-quality brain, Momma got me things and spoke like I was half as smart as Matty. She instructed me not to fall asleep. Pronouncing each word ultra-clear, she explained that sleeping can kill somebody with a head injury.

"I won't sleep."

As if I was three years old, she brushed hair out of my face and soft as a breeze promised that everything was all right, that the voices could be controlled with medication and that she had scheduled a doctor's appointment for me early in the week. That's when I asked her how long it would take for the anti-voice medication to make me normal. I was thinking that if a couple of days would do the trick, people at school, including Daisy, wouldn't have to know anything about my problem.

Seated on the edge of my bed, Momma said, "It can take a while to get the meds balanced properly. It can take a month or a year or even a few years. And . . . and they aren't easy on people. They can be a burden. It all depends on the severity of the illness, and that can range." She touched one of her crabbish hands to my pasty forehead. "We won't worry about that right now. No one even knows for sure that you've got schizophrenia. Tests need to be run. Evaluations need to be made. We're at the very beginning of a long process."

I rolled away from her. "I'm tired of this shit already."

"Don't cuss," Momma directed limply. With an exhausted grunt, she rose off Granddad Penrod's old bed and stared down at me. Behind her silver head, the amoeba water stains on my slanted ceiling reminded me of freckly spots on old people's faces. Momma said, "Penn, I'm so sorry. I'd give anything to make this go away. I would."

"Yeah," I answered, not wanting her to cry. "Well, don't worry. It's not gonna take a few months," I said. "I'm gonna be fine." But I wasn't sure I would be.

When she left, I sat in bed watching television till it got so awful I couldn't stand it. Cutting it off, I got out basketball magazines of Matty's, curled around my pillow, and read. Around two-thirty, after school was out, Hurlee called.

"Dude, they said ya threw a desk across the room."

My head began to throb. "I fell is all."

He stayed quiet, so that I wondered if the phone line had died.

"Hurlee?"

"Yo."

Softly, so as not to cause my tender brain to hurt, I asked, "What's up?"

"Nothing, 'cept I don't know what's going on. Kid says ya was talking to people who weren't in the room. That's what he said."

"Well, I wasn't. I was talking to the class."

Hurlee was quiet before saying, "Hey, I gotta go. We gonna meet at the Citgo. Everybody be asking 'bout ya."

"Tell 'em I'm okay."

"All right, dude."

"I wasn't talking to myself, either."

"Didn't think so, man."

I hung up the phone and rubbed at my temples. I wished Daisy would call and waited patiently till after five o'clock. By then, I knew she wouldn't.

As darkness fell across Havre de Grace, a storm

slipped in so that fog and rain clouded and clung, like plastic sheets, to the trees and wires outside. Dad arrived home from delivering my newspapers and after talking to Momma, came upstairs. He winked at me and went about placing buckets and pans to catch water dripping through our patched roof.

Finished, he wandered about till he got to the side of my bed. As if I was dying of a terminal disease, he sat down slow and proceeded to collapse against me and spend ten minutes blubbering on one of my shoulders. Smelling of wet cement, he told me how proud he was to be my father. Wiping and wiping a grimy hand over his slick head, he asked if I knew how much he respected the way I acted with Matty.

"I guess."

"Good. 'Cause I do respect that. I really do."

Before dinner, Matty got home, came up the steps, and peeked into my room. He blinked a bunch of times and asked, "Penn, what'd you do?"

"Hit my head."

"Does it hurt?"

"Yeah."

He propped himself in my doorway and stuck his hands in the pockets of his Burger King pants.

"What?" I asked.

"Are you real sick?"

"No."

"Momma and Dad are acting like you are."

"So?"

"What do you got?"

"Nothing. It's nothing but the voices I was hearing. They mean I got a minor sickness. But you don't have to worry—you can't catch it."

"I want to."

Adjusting my pillow, I said, "It's so idiotic, you would hate it."

"But I want to have it, too. So that you don't have to be all alone."

I frowned at him.

"It's just true."

Downstairs, there was a hard knock on the front door.

"Somebody's here," he informed me.

"Matty, I got ears." My gaze veered toward *Wheel of Fortune,* playing on the old black-and-white television. I watched somebody spin the wheel. Then it occurred to me that Daisy might be the person at the door. Swinging about, I said to Matty, "Hey, go look down and tell me if a girl's visiting. Be sneaky. Don't act like you're doing it."

"But I was just gonna use the bathroom."

"Check first." I ran my fingers through my hair to

make it straighter. Trying to get a feel for my breath, I panted into the other hand and breathed deep with my nostrils. I couldn't tell anything.

Matty slid along the hallway wall and angled his head around the corner. He retreated in a similar, slithery way. "It's not a girl. It's Uncle Hewitt."

"It is?"

"Yeah."

I threw my pillow across the room.

"What?"

"Nothing."

"You wanted it to be a girl?"

"I wanted it to be Daisy."

Matty held tight to one of his elbows, his expression changing quickly to one of extreme discomfort. "I really gotta use the toilet," he told me, "then I'll come back."

"Go on," I growled, standing unsteadily. I slapped the television off, picked up my pillow, and fell onto my bed just as people started up the steps.

Flipping over, I glowered at the door.

Dad and Uncle Hewitt got to the top of the landing and veered into my room. The floorboards creaked from their weight. Neither looked at me. Both stopped, then stepped and stopped again. I remembered how, in Canvasback's, a voice had said that Uncle Hewitt was causing my problems. Recollecting that got me edgy.

Dad put his hands in his pockets and spoke. "Uncle Hewitt says he'd like to talk with you. You wanna talk with him?"

"I don't care."

"He says he understands how you feel."

I laughed, causing my head to ache. "No he doesn't."

Uncle Hewitt told me, "Back when I was the police chief, I had a way of soothing ruffled nerves, and I can't imagine ya got anything but those right now. That's why I wanna help." He grinned so that his yellowish teeth were visible.

Dad said, "Penn, all I wanna know is if you feel like talking."

I said, "I can talk."

Uncle Hewitt leaned his rear against my desk. "I'll only be a few minutes."

Dad left us alone.

I told Uncle Hewitt, "You're sort of making my room smell like cigarettes and liquor."

"It's 'cause I ain't fresh." He looked at the ceiling, and his stringy white hair piled against his collar. "Yer roof is leaking something awful."

"It's been doing that since my dad got it patched."

Unhurried, he roamed over to the window and extended his hands to warm them over the radiator.

"So, what are you gonna tell me?"

"Gonna give ya the scoop as to what ya got, Penrod." Turning slow, he peered at me in a sad, sad way, right through the curls of his heavy, whitish eyebrows.

I stared back.

"Came 'cause I was at a bar and heard what happened. Heard ya was talking to yerself. It's all over town. Ya was having a conversation with ghosts or something."

Hearing the word "ghost" caused my jaw to tremble.

"Feel sorry for what you're going through. If I'd seen it earlier, I coulda helped. But it wasn't till the other night before I realized things."

Lightheaded and distant from myself, I asked, "Am I having a nightmare?"

"Feels that way, but ya ain't."

Out in the hallway, Matty came banging out of the bathroom door. "Hey, Uncle Hewitt," he boomed.

Rough as sandpaper, Uncle Hewitt replied, "Good to see ya, Matthew. Now, ya do me a favor and go on downstairs. Me and your brother got serious business together."

Chapter Eight

Penrod," Uncle Hewitt said, "What do ya know 'bout me aside from I'm yer uncle?"

I whispered, "You were police chief and quit on the day Aunt Birdy died."

He winced.

"You drink a lot and wander around town."

"True," he said, like it was difficult to hear. Circling, he put his hands over my radiator again. "When I was yer age, somebody told me I might be a bum or a lunatic when I got older, and I guess botha those predictions came true, didn't they?" He scowled, and his teeth flashed their yellowness in the ceiling light. He leaned down and put his face against my radiator, warming a cheek and his rubbery neck.

From that awkward, sideways position, he said, "Christ, Penrod, I been cold lately. God-damned weather turned so that my old bones don't wanna get the chill out." Placing one side of his nose against a fin of the radiator, he closed his eyes and enjoyed the heat.

I scooted to the edge of my bed and put my feet wide on the floor, like I was trying to gain balance on a shifting boat. Around us, water plopped into pots and pans.

He said, "Nothing makes sense, does it?"

"No, sir."

With a tiny grunt, he lifted his weathered head. "Don't call me sir. Call me Uncle Hewitt or plain Hewitt. I'm just a bum, Penrod. Ya can see that. Right now, at this point in our lives, ya deserve more respect than me."

Being that I wasn't a bum, I nodded agreement.

Uncle Hewitt snickered. "Yeah. Yup, yup. You're right."

"Right about what?"

"Everything. I'm a bum and ya ain't. You're right. I been one so long, I don't ask for respect. I had it and quit on it. I ain't making excuses." He straightened and looked at me sternly. "You ready for what I'm about to say?"

"I guess."

"You sure?"

"Maybe."

"Okay, then, Penrod. Here and now and without a doubt, ya ain't sick. I know ya ain't."

"Mom thinks I am."

"She's wrong, boy. You're completely regular for the type of person ya happen to be." Unzipping his nylon jacket, Uncle Hewitt fluttered it, sending water all over my furniture, sheets, and floor before he rested it across my garbage can.

"I'm hearing voices."

Hewitt smoothed his wild white eyebrows. Done, he put an index finger to his lips and hushed me. "I know. All of Havre de Grace knows. Ya . . . ya gotta be more quiet about it. It ain't safe. Let me explain something, Penrod. You're hearing voices, that's true. You're hearing 'em all right. What I mean is, ya got a magical trick about you. Ya got the curse'a hearing other people's thoughts."

Feeling bleary, I said, "Momma told me it might be schizophrenia."

He laughed. "That's what she thinks, but it ain't. It's something other than that." Uncle Hewitt seated himself alongside me. "I been through this. I been told I was sick. Felt exactly the way ya do right now. Believe me, I know."

Silently, I thought he was insane but hoped he

wasn't, which was hard considering all the years I'd seen him as a staggering bum. Those were hard to forget. Still, he recognized my experiences and had once been respectable, I reminded myself. He'd been an important man in town.

"Looky here," he said, "Ya can't worry 'bout it. What ya got is as natural as growing up. It's like the way a beard grows."

I touched my face and wondered if he'd read my thoughts. "I've been thinking about beards."

He tapped his head. Standing with a jolt, he went over and examined my poster of the man stepping out of a window, into the sky. "What a dope," he commented. He wrinkled his nose and clicked his tongue. He wheeled around like a top that's losing speed. "Give my regards to the cook, Penrod. I'm gonna go. I'm gonna get a drink and a cigarette and think about other things. But we're gonna be talking a lot. We're gonna spend a lotta time together, and I ain't even gonna charge ya a penny."

"I . . . I got other things I need to do."

He shook his head. "Not other things that're more important." He leaned forward and whispered, "Let me give ya some advice, when the voices come, stay calm. The thing is not to fight. If ya wanna ignore 'em, ya do it like when you're watching television and somebody says something to ya and ya don't listen. That's it. Understand?"

"I guess."

He put his hands in his pockets. "Last of all, don't ya tell a soul what I said till ya know ya can trust 'em. If other people found out 'bout you, there'd be hell to pay. There'd be mass hysteria. And especially don't tell nobody in the psychological field. They're close-minded assholes . . . 'cept for yer momma, of course. Understand? We gotta be cautious folk, and shrinks are blabbermouths who wanna shove awful medicines down your throat. You stay quiet."

"I won't say stuff," I assured him, drawn to his belief that I was becoming special and not crazy. I told myself that the voices always had divulged people's secrets, like I was talking with their spirits. The first time I'd heard one, I'd known that Matty was worrying I might die from cigarettes. The second time, I'd learned how Momma thought Dad was a fat whiner. And just that morning, I'd discovered that Ms. Lang was burned out from teaching. I'd heard true things.

Uncle Hewitt smiled and drew a shaking hand from a pocket. "Welcome to the club. And don't ya worry. I'm gonna help ya through. I ain't one for fate, neither. I ain't one for lofty crap like that no more. But I suppose I could be alive and living my sorry life for a reason. I suppose."

Bleary, I said, "My parents think the worst."

"Course they do. Thing is, in time, I'm gonna explain it to them."

On his way to the stairs, Uncle Hewitt swerved over to my wastepaper basket and snatched up his wet windbreaker. Squeezing it tight in the middle, he looked like he was holding a big ribbon, a present. "We'll see each other in a few days. I'll find ya."

He didn't look back. Holding the rail, he took the stairs cautiously, like he was wearing roller skates. Still, as small and wobbly as he was, I could almost imagine him as Havre de Grace's upstanding and heroic police chief.

After Uncle Hewitt left, Momma and Dad creaked up the stairs and dallied about my room with intense looks on their faces.

I said, "Thanks for letting him in."

Momma glared at my father. "It wasn't me."

"Penn," Dad said thoughtfully, "Uncle Hewitt wants to help. I didn't see the harm. He holds a pretty interesting conversation, and despite how he looks, he's a smart man. Least he was."

"He still is," I said. "He told me good news, too. It's that he doesn't think I got schizophrenia. He says it's something else."

"What?" Momma asked.

"He thinks I'm okay."

She shivered once, so bad I thought of a tuning fork. "Penn, dear," she mumbled.

Dad told me, "He was trying to calm your nerves. That's all."

Momma put the backside of a hand against my jaw. "I appreciate that Uncle Hewitt means well, but he's been out of touch since Aunt Birdy died. The issue is not one that he understands. I'm sorry." She sat down beside me and shivered once more. "I wish it was true. I want it as bad as I've ever wanted anything. If I could undo your problem, it'd be done. Your uncle, Penn, he doesn't understand."

I turned my head from her. "He understands," I wanted to say, but couldn't. I knew he was unstable but wanted to believe what he'd said. After all, I told myself, he'd known that I'd been trying to grow my beard. I hadn't said a word. He'd given me some proof.

In old Havre de Grace, way before I was born, people worked on Saturdays. They scampered into their fishing boats or carried off their duck guns like it was a standard day of the week. Not now. These days, except for folks who run stores, everybody in town takes Saturday off, including the writers and printers at the *Havre de Grace Morning Document*. So, after whacking my head at school on Friday morning, I was able to sit at home healing Saturday without missing another paper delivery. I was lucky and spent the time considering Uncle Hewitt's visit and how much I missed Daisy. Both subjects got me tired.

On Sunday, I woke up feeling like I'd never had a concussion. In the afternoon, I delivered my papers as usual, then I came home and watched football games with my dad.

During the late game, just wanting to talk, I said, "They're a good match for the Ravens."

"They're all right."

"Sometimes, I like watching football a lot more than other times. Do you?"

"Course," he answered. "'Specially with my number-two son."

Outside, the wind blew hard, shaking mostly bare trees and throwing a dust storm of dried leaves into the air. I loved that. I thought back to when me and Matty were younger and how he'd rake piles of leaves together so I could jump into them off a stepladder.

On a long run from scrimmage, my father lunged forward excitedly, spilling his bowl of low-fat potato chips. "Ravens're pulling away!" he told me. It wasn't till he sat back that he noticed the mess in his lap.

"You spilled when you threw your hands in the air."

"Well, it's worth it. It's great, huh?"

Momma came in and sat on the sofa beside me. She watched the game for a few minutes and asked, "You okay?"

"Okay enough."

"Good." She sat for a while longer, then she rose and left the room, wandering slowly toward the kitchen.

My father glanced over at me. "Let's not talk about any of your problems. Is that all right with you?"

"Dad, I'd like never to talk about them again." And I hoped I never would have to, either.

Chapter Nine

The next morning, I felt akin to a flattened pigeon that I had seen downtown the day before. I crawled from Granddad Penrod's old bed feeling gloomy and wondering what terrible events the week would hold.

In the kitchen, I said, "Do I have an appointment today?"

Momma said, "Soonest I could get was Wednesday morning."

I started loading my book bag.

She asked, "What're you doing?"

"Getting ready for school."

"I don't think so."

I stared at her. "Why not?"

She bit at her bottom lip. "I figured you'd stay home." She polished her forehead with a palm. "You don't feel sick?"

"I feel completely usual."

"You want to go to school?"

"Real badly."

She nodded. "Okay, Penn. Okay, sweetie."

Twenty minutes later, breathing cloud-banks of steam, Momma and I climbed into the car. She started the engine and let it warm as she fixed her lipstick and eyes in the rearview mirror. Without saying a word, she backed onto Union Avenue and shifted gears. The car sputtered and out from the tailpipe erupted a thunderhead of blue smoke. Momma didn't see the cloud, but I suppose I should've pointed it out to her. We got about three blocks before the car broke down. Drifting to a stop in front of the hospital, we abandoned it and started walking.

In the principal's leathery, plush office, my mother explained, "He's getting a psychological evaluation on Wednesday and probably some tests will be run. I don't know for certain. But he wants to be in school."

Mr. Stevenson smiled. He and my momma had

known each other since they were kids. Growing up, he'd been her crybaby neighbor whose parents dressed him funny. "Belinda, I know you understand the seriousness of what happened. It frightened numerous students. Furthermore, teachers are not paid to baby-sit. I'm not sure I . . ."

"Mr. Stevenson?"

"Belinda?"

Momma straightened. "My son can watch out for himself."

"So you think, but . . ."

"Mr. Stevenson, I realize that Penn doesn't dress the way you want. I am aware that his peers are not valedictorians, but he's a good kid who works hard. He's going through a very difficult time and wants to be in school. He wants to learn. Are you denying him that right?"

Mr. Stevenson studied the calendar blotter on his enormous, glossy desk. His hands tinkered together. "No, Belinda. No, I am not suggesting we deny him anything, but . . ."

"I didn't think so."

Mr. Stevenson leaned back. "He could get teased."

"Who cares," I said, even though I'd hate that.

"I'll have to tell his teachers," he told Momma. Looking at me, he said, "I'll have to tell your teachers."

"Go ahead."

"Do what's necessary," Momma agreed, standing. She gave him her business card. "Call me immediately if there are any problems."

He nodded.

Momma turned to me. "Penn, you let someone know if you experience any troubles, any at all. This afternoon, wait for your father if you don't feel like delivering your papers."

"I'll be all right."

Mr. Stevenson sent me into the front office so that they could have a private conversation, then Momma left.

In algebra, I took my usual desk, the students giving me sideways glances like I'd risen from the grave.

Ms. Lang said, "Welcome back, Penn. We worried about you."

"Thanks, ma'am," I replied. But I wondered how she really felt and remembered the nasty things her voice had said before I hit my head.

When the bell clanged, I rushed out the door and through school, from algebra to history, my stomach rumbling with so much gas I imagined floating to the ceiling and getting stuck, like a drugstore balloon, beside a light fixture. At the classroom door, I peeked in and saw that Daisy hadn't arrived. Relieved, I darted to my desk and sat with my head down over my notebook, waiting for class to start.

When the bell rang, our history teacher welcomed me back with a nod. The man's upper lip twitched, as usual, and he started in on our lesson, talking and talking about strikes and protests and a march on Washington where military veterans camped by the United States Capitol building. Throughout, I kept my eyes zeroed in on the blackboard, even though, from the very corner of my eye, I could see Daisy moving and wanted to look at her so bad. I didn't. I refused. It would've been awful to see her try to avoid me.

Regardless, the first time our teacher asked a question and called on Daisy to answer, out of habit, I glanced over. Our eyes connected, and she told our teacher, "Douglas MacArthur."

Biting on my pencil eraser, I felt soaked in misery.

Daisy answered another question by saying, "Bonus Army," and when I peeked again, her dark eyes pounded me like a hammer.

Class over, she headed me off at the front of the room. Even though I was scared to talk, I was glad she did it since she was the whole reason I'd returned to school instead of exploiting my mental glitch and taking the week off.

"Penn?"

"Hey."

"I thought you were sick."

"I'm better." I pulled on my three whiskers as we went out into the hallway. I could see the fire in her magnified eyes and felt like I had to say more, to apologize for fainting. "I . . . I guess what I did on Friday embarrassed you, huh?"

Daisy tilted her head. "How'd it embarrass me?"

"I fainted."

"That's what you think, that I'm embarrassed?"

"Well, you didn't call."

"You mean, you didn't call me. I gave you my phone number; you didn't give me yours."

I felt the weight of my stupidity flop like a wet towel over my shoulders. "Oh, yeah."

All around us, students squeezed past, watching me intensely.

I asked, "Did . . . did you want me to call?"

"Of course."

I waited a moment, then said, "But, Daisy, think about it. If you hang out with me, people'll say things."

"So?"

Stepping back, I leaned against the doorframe to our

class. "Over the weekend, I wanted to talk to you real badly. I tried to remember how your voice sounded."

She nodded. "Penn, I've got to get to class. But you're coming to lunch, right?"

"Yeah," I answered, so relieved that she still liked me, I could've fallen on the floor and gotten trampled and it would've been all right.

That afternoon, I walked Daisy home to the Water's Edge Condominiums. Halfway, she wrangled her hand in mine, causing me to feel sort of weak and keyed up at the same time.

Softly, she told me what it was like living outside of Oakland and San Francisco on rolling, rolling hills that made everything look similar to a giant, hugely wrinkled carpet of fake grass. She explained that her dad had joined the Navy when he was a teenager in the Philippines and how he had worked his way up slowly, gone to school, earned an engineering degree, and become an officer. In fact, her parents put a lot of pressure on her to succeed. "It's a first generation thing," she said.

"My mother and father don't put much pressure on me. Though Momma does say I'm lazy."

A moment passed. "You don't seem lazy."

"I am."

Daisy glanced at me. "You seem smart."

"Only in history," I told her before changing the subject. "Do your relatives ever come over here to visit?"

"My mom's parents and siblings don't travel."

"Are they too poor?"

"No," she laughed. "They don't want to. Besides, they like where they are. They've got a big house and some cars." She let go of my hand and walked ahead, speaking over her shoulder. "They aren't rich, you're right. I mean, the last time my mother was there, my grandfather still made toilet tissue from strips of newspaper."

"No way."

"Toilet paper costs too much."

I wondered how expensive a roll could be since I'd pay an awful lot before using newspaper. "How about your dad's parents?"

"Both of them are dead."

"That's sad," I said.

We stopped at the gates to Daisy's condominium. Because I didn't know how to say goodbye to a girlfriend, I tried to look busy, kicking rocks over the curb a few times. Then Daisy stood right in front of me so that I couldn't move away. Watching myself in her glasses, I leaned over and we kissed. This time, her puffy lips stayed on mine a little longer, so that it seemed like electricity passed between us.

"I don't wanna go, but I gotta deliver my papers."

"Maybe I can come with you tomorrow."

"You always can." I reached into one of my back pockets and drew out the slip of paper I'd scratched my phone number on. "Now you can call me."

"Good."

"Yeah."

"So, are you okay?"

I paused. "I'm fine. They're . . . they're gonna run some tests, is all." I kissed her once more and left, which was real hard to do. I felt attached, almost sewn. The farther away I got from her, the harder the threads pulled.

At home, I dumped my book bag, then ran downtown, past the closed-down shops, my grandparents' old hardware store, and Totally Cowboy. Rushing into the *Havre de Grace Morning Document* offices, I called hello to Rhonda and went about hauling my papers outside. On the sidewalk, I carefully rolled each especially fat copy, crammed with frozen turkey coupons and gravy ads. As I worked, I looked about and imagined me and Daisy returning to Havre de Grace after going to college. We could live near my parents and Matty and visit whenever we felt like it. It would be perfect.

Done, I heaved my sack over a shoulder, got balanced, and started up the sidewalk.

"Penrod!" Uncle Hewitt's familiar, rough voice called from down the street.

I turned about as he struggled along toward me, his pant legs and shoes covered in dark smudges like chimney soot. A cracked vinyl belt flopped loose at his hip. Rising over that was the windbreaker he'd worn a few nights before.

"Can I come along?"

He looked so terrible I was embarrassed to be seen with him.

"We gotta talk about your problem," he explained, swiping at his thin hair, a strip of which had dropped down and poked him in an eye, forcing him to squint. "And I know I look awful. I agree, but nobody's gonna care, neither."

He'd known what I was thinking, and I was glad for that. Still, I said, "Uncle Hewitt, Momma thinks you're crazy."

"Well, it might seem so, but I ain't. Think about it, Penrod. Think about how I never once drew my gun on any of the fools I had to deal with in my time on the force. It's 'cause I knew things, is how. I had my edge. On account of knowing their thoughts, I could talk 'em outta anything."

I smiled. It seemed like he might be telling the truth.

We shuffled up the street, stopping at Union Avenue,

alongside the fire station and the old opera house that's become an empty building. We waited to cross the busy roadway, and a blast of cold wind ran leaves about our feet. Way up, traveling slowly in the bumpy air, a military plane veered in the thin white light. I squinted at its camouflaged sides for a second, as it moved in front of the sun, then I looked behind me, toward the water, where I found the plane's shadow skimming along the mouth of the Susquehanna River, like a whale just beneath the surface.

Uncle Hewitt reached into a pocket of his windbreaker and found a bent cigarette.

We crossed the street, and I tossed a few papers then turned and walked backwards. "Are you gonna tell me things?"

"What do ya want ta know, Penrod?"

"What's going on with me. And . . . and if what you said is true."

He scratched his greasy scalp. "Well, to be honest, I don't rightly understand our hearing-thoughts situation myself. Nobody does. Nobody's ever done research on it. But the fact is, you gotta recognize that I couldn't make it up. You hear what you hear."

He was right about that. I got another paper loose from the bag. Hoping that the ridiculous was possible, I twisted the paper and lobbed it onto a front porch. Maybe my future wasn't going to be so terrible after all.

"Penrod, ya gotta know you're magical. Do you see?"

I adjusted the bag on my shoulder. "I suppose," I told him, but I wasn't completely convinced even though I wanted to be.

Uncle Hewitt grinned and stayed quiet for a few blocks. Then, for some reason, he said, "By the by, your momma's parents were good folk. Was sorry to see 'em leave for Florida. Your momma musta been awfully sad."

"She didn't say."

"Well, I know she was."

It was a relief to think that he'd read her mind and knew more than I did. Far off, muffled explosions rumbled from the Aberdeen Proving Grounds. They reminded me of Daisy's father. I said to Hewitt, "Did you know I'm getting a girlfriend?"

"I knew."

"You did?"

"Sure."

I waited a second before saying, "Is she a nice girl?"

"She's nice."

I stopped and decided to test him some more. "You know what country she's from?"

"Just America, huh?"

His comment reminded me that Daisy didn't like

people to think of her as a foreigner. "I always forget that she was born here."

"That's right."

I watched his face. "You really do read minds, don't you?"

"I wouldn't lie to ya, Penrod, not about something like that."

A while later, for fear of getting spotted, I skirted Revolution Street and my friends at the closed Citgo gas station. I didn't want them to question my mental steadiness any more than they already did, and if they saw me stumbling along with my wild-seeming uncle, they would. Instead, we short-cutted a block over and shuffled down Lafayette Street, back onto Union Avenue, where I tossed one of my remaining papers.

Behind me, Hewitt took a long breath and put his hands on his knees.

I asked, "You all right?"

"Oh, yeah. All right, enough." Straightening, he snuffed the remains of what was likely his tenth cigarette on a half-charred spot of his khaki pants. Reaching down, he massaged his sore legs. "Penrod, ya got a long, strange road ahead."

"Do I?"

"Oh, yeah. Ya gotta maintain the courage of your

convictions all the way down it, too. Ya gotta tell yourself that what I'm telling you is true."

I nodded. "Does it have a name?"

He stared at me. "Yeah. Of course, it's Pygmy Syndrome."

"Pygmy Syndrome?"

He hushed me. "Not too loud. There're people who'd pay good money to find out about us."

I looked around at the empty streets before saying, "Why's it called that?"

"Simple reason. Pygmy means small, and everyone who's got it's a pip-squeak. None of us grows much. It's like whatever gives us what we got stops us from getting tall. Hate to tell ya, but ya won't get much taller than ya already are. Matter fact, I bet ya don't grow another inch. I stopped when I was thirteen. Just stopped cold in my tracks and never grew again."

I was horrified.

"Who the hell cares about being short? Nobody does," said Uncle Hewitt.

"I do."

"Yeah, I can tell. Get used to it. Tallest Pygmy I know is five-foot-six. We don't come no bigger."

I dropped my newspaper sack to the ground. "Shit!" I said, and kicked at it. "I always counted on getting taller. I counted on it."

"Can't count on nothing, can you, Penrod?"

I glared down at my feet, at my shoes, and it occurred to me that I'd worn the same size for two years.

Hewitt grinned. "Gonna be okay. It will be. Ya digest that information and I'll go ahead and leave." He put his hands in his pants pockets. "Ya tell your parents I'll be 'round. Tell 'em I wanna talk some more. But don't tell 'em what you got. Not yet."

I refused to reply since I already had leaked his earlier information.

"Penrod, come on, the height thing don't matter. Forget about it."

I snapped, "I never wanted to be a small person."

"You'll get used to it."

Chapter Ten

After Uncle Hewitt left, I tried not to think about Pygmy Syndrome but found the idea kind of unsettling. So, as an alternative, I decided to consider Daisy. Mostly, I thought about our future together. I wondered if we had one and what made certain relationships last while others crumbled. I thought back over my own extended family. My great-granddad Cleon had stayed married for fifty years, while my granddad Penrod got dumped by his wife while he was still in his thirties. My parents were still together, but they weren't exactly all over each other. Instead, it seemed like they'd sort of surrendered to their different personality issues.

Considering all the way home, I took a seat in the kitchen across from Matty. Dad was drinking a beer and Momma was cooking, so I asked them how people stay together.

"It's hard to say," Momma replied as she cooked. "It might be blind luck."

Dad said, "Blind luck and a willingness to forgive."

It didn't seem right that relationships were based on luck and forgiveness. I picked at a fingernail and thought a moment. Then I said, "You remember how Great-Granddad Cleon could carve decoys? You think Grandma liked that? You think she thought he was an artistic genius or something?"

Dad smiled. "Maybe."

I looked away. "Yeah, I wish I could carve."

"Try it," Dad offered. "I did, once, when I was about your age, and I nearly hacked off the top of this finger. See how it's bent funny?"

"How'd that happen?"

"With a chisel."

Matty mumbled, "Must've hurt."

"Oh, yeah," Dad said.

Momma jiggled a pan of chicken, causing a crackle of grease to fly. "Penn, why the sudden concern?"

"Because."

"Because what?"

"I don't know."

Matty squinted at me as if peeking through bifocals. "Is it 'cause of Daisy?"

Momma turned. "Daisy?"

Dad quit guzzling his beer.

"God, Matty, sometimes you can't remember anything, and other times you don't ever forget." I glanced at my parents.

"Who's Daisy?" Momma asked.

I stood and leaned against the back of the chair. "It's my personal business, but if you've got to know, she's my girlfriend." I paused. "She's like the smartest person in school, and I want her to be interested in me for a while. You know? That's why I was thinking about relationships. I was trying to figure out why Grandmomma got tired of Granddad Penrod, and wondered if it was because he didn't have any talent or something. Maybe he was a bore?"

My father said, "He played the harmonica pretty good. It just didn't work out. They were different people."

Momma added, "Also, he had a wandering eye."

Dad nodded and lowered his empty beer bottle to his leg, where he bounced it softly against one of his wide thighs.

I said, "It must've been interesting to see how Great-Granddad Cleon could carve."

"Probably was."

I glanced down at the table and studied Matty, then I put a hand on one of his shoulders. I wasn't actually mad at him for squealing about Daisy. I didn't mind my parents knowing. It made me feel adult and complex and less crazy.

Dad plunked his bottle on the counter. He wandered over and looked at the chicken, then returned. "Penn, I'm wondering, you think it's a good time for you to have a girlfriend?"

My mother rotated around. "I don't believe it is."

"Yeah, it is," I answered. "It's the perfect time."

Momma swiveled back.

Dad shifted his weight from one knee to the other. Reaching up, he spun his bottle atop the counter and caught it before it toppled. "We're worried about you, Penn. We aren't trying to ruin anything. We want you to be happy."

"She makes me happy."

"She's smart?" Momma asked.

"She can answer every question in history. I'm not even exaggerating."

"Does she know what's been happening to you?"

"No," I admitted. But what I wanted to say to Momma was that I wasn't schizophrenic, that I was actually a Pygmy instead.

"You don't think she ought to hear about it, Penn?"

115

"I don't think," I said, irritated by the idea.

Momma returned to her frying pan. "Well, if you don't tell her, and you check into a hospital, she might have a hard time contacting you, huh?"

"If I go somewhere, I'm gonna tell her it's for a vacation."

In the middle of the night, I dreamed of tall pine trees with tips that disappeared into soft white clouds floating miles overhead. There was Daisy, looking gorgeous, seated on the branch of one tree. Above her was Matty, and he wasn't retarded anymore. I smiled, lurched, and found my mother and father seated in a field of flowers and holding tight to each other without a hint of stress or strain between them. It was like heaven. Then heaven began to change, and voices nagged and nagged till I woke.

Sitting up, I peered out my window at a tatter of dark clouds floating in front of the stars and across the moon, which had a small dent in the top. Meanwhile, a spray of conversation shot through my head like the fragments of a Havre de Grace house that had exploded from a faulty gas line. Unafraid for the first time, I listened before concentrating on the loudest voice, which happened to be a lady's. "What're you saying?" "What're you talking about?" I kept asking it.

The voice replied, saying it was heartbreakingly sad. "Who are you?"

"Mrs. Mitchell, your neighbor, whose husband died last year."

"Hey, Mrs. Mitchell."

"Hello," Mrs. Mitchell said. "If you want to know why I'm heartbreakingly sad, I'll tell you. I miss him, Mr. Mitchell. He was everything to me, and now he's gone. Now I've got nothing."

"When I was little, you guys rode around town on yellow scooters."

"Wasn't that grand?" she said. "It was, which makes being alone even worse, especially during Thanksgiving week."

"Call your kids."

"They've got their own families to care for."

"But they'd want to know you're sad."

"No. Nobody cares, Penn. Nobody."

I thought about the way she dismissed everyone and asked, "Are you depressed?"

"Depressed?"

"Super-sad or something."

"Well, yes, I believe so. I do believe I am super-sad."

"Then you gotta get help."

She didn't reply, but I wasn't going to forget about it.

Momma had explained depression to me, and I knew how dangerous it was. "Mrs. Mitchell?"

"Yes."

"You gotta get help."

"I . . . I suppose you're right."

"I am."

"Penn, it's just that sometimes I feel like quitting. Why not? That's how I feel. I feel like I might hurt myself."

I sat forward. "Well, you can't do it."

"I can. I hate to say it, but I can."

"Not now that I know."

"I am sorry for that," she said. "I shouldn't have told you."

"Well, I won't let you hurt yourself," I said. Feeling desperate, I lunged at her sadness and got my thoughts around it. It took a minute to get a firm hold, but I did and began tugging her pain toward me and away from her. "I'm gonna save you, Mrs. Mitchell."

Sweat started dripping down my head, and my legs roasted as if I had a fever. Still, I pulled till her sadness began to tear slowly away and shake out into my brain. When I was through, I felt as bleak and hopeless as a drifting iceberg, while she felt so much better that her voice sputtered away like a balloon that's not tied off. In an instant, other voices took her place, but hearing them

118

didn't help. I was alone like a person without friends and a shameful history of mistakes.

The next morning, nothing seemed worth doing. Downstairs, even though I wasn't hungry, I ate for Momma, who was making no bones about monitoring me.

"You don't look good," she said after a few minutes.

Matty told her, "Except for having a stuffed nose, I'm okay."

"I'm talking to your brother, sweetie."

"I feel so good I wanna scream," I told her sarcastically, trying to sound like I did when I was normal.

She dipped her head and her lips touched against her coffee cup.

I took a big, nauseating bite of corn puffs. "I stayed up late doing school work."

Momma nodded but appeared suspicious.

I got up. "I'm meeting Daisy," I lied so that I could leave early.

On the sidewalk, steam billowed from my mouth as if I was an old locomotive making for a mountain. At the intersection of Lafayette Street and Union Avenue, I checked behind me to make sure I wasn't being followed, then I went in the opposite direction. Above, the sun twinkled bright in an ugly, bleachy way, while all around the wind yowled hard, rustling small piles of garbage and leaves together. Everywhere I looked, Havre de Grace seemed absolutely doomed by a bleak history and a similar future.

Hurrying south along Market Street, I searched down the hill, above the rooftops of houses and old buildings, to the shore, where the bay was covered in flashing whitecaps that caused a couple of distant geese and seagulls to rise and fall as if they were floating Clorox bottles. I kept staring, nearly hypnotized, till I arrived in front of Uncle Hewitt's place.

Momma says that prior to Aunt Birdy's accident, Uncle Hewitt's home had been kept nice. As far back as I could remember, though, it hadn't been. Not that the houses around it were breathtaking. They weren't by a long stretch, but Hewitt's stuck out for its general junkiness. Covered with warping, weathered asbestos shingles, it drooped like a cheap tent with bent poles. Broken shutters banged against windows that were missing panes of glass, and the surrounding yard was all overgrown weeds and grass that was thick enough to stash washers and dryers in. The old shrubs circling the foundation were wild and halfway dead, packed with about ten birds' nests and candy wrappers that whistled in the breeze.

Passing between the weeds, I went up the bendy steps and shuffled across the porch. I knocked on the front door and waited. After a bit, I banged harder, dislodging wide curls of red paint, and causing the door to unlatch and swing wide. Leaning into the filthy hallway, I called for Uncle Hewitt. Cautious, I stepped inside and peeked into the dusty dining room. I turned and searched in the dark den, across the nearly blank walls and empty, stuffed and stained furniture. My eyes got to the couch, and I spotted what looked like a flea-baggy dog stirring slightly. Squinting through the darkness, I shuffled closer and realized it was Uncle Hewitt, slumped into a pillow and curled like a baby. Cold as it was in there, he didn't have a shirt on. He was naked down to his grubby khaki pants.

"Uncle Hewitt?" I said, loudly, trying not to smell the stale air.

Sniffling, he cracked open his pouchy eyes. When he saw me, he scooted up, his naked chest gleaming in a way that reminded me of the frozen turkey my mother had bought. He put his flat toes to the dusty floor and tried to focus. "Penrod?" he croaked.

"Hey."

"Ya don't respect privacy?"

"I do."

"Well, go on and tell me what'cha want, so ya can get."

"You can't tell?"

"Tell what?"

"What I want?"

"No," he mumbled. "Too tired to make my brain focus. Just go on and tell me. "

I shivered. "I did something weird last night."

"Cough it up." He grabbed a dirty white T-shirt and yanked it over his head.

"I don't exactly know what it was."

"Explain it, then."

I took a second to put together my thoughts, and said, "Uncle Hewitt, I . . . I woke up hearing people, like Pygmies do. The thing is, I started asking the loudest voice questions and found out it belonged to our neighbor, who, it turns out, is really depressed. She misses her husband who died last year, and her grownup kids don't visit." I swallowed. "I guess I wanted to help, so I took her sadness from her and put it in me. I got it in me, and now it's not going away."

Hewitt cocked his head, startled. "Ya took her mood?"

"I did, yeah. I just did 'cause I could, and she needed help."

Hewitt stood. His shaking hands strayed about his sides. "Christ almighty, Penrod, most Pygmies can't ever do that. Most can't. Only the strongest, the . . . ah . . . kings, and they're all gone now. That's why . . . that's why I didn't warn ya 'bout it."

"I got the worst sadness," I said, leaning against a chair. "I . . . I did it to make her feel better. I didn't know I'd get depressed, too."

Hewitt straggled about the room, stopping in front of a curling photo pinned in the middle of a large wall. He put his hands on both sides of it, leaned, and kissed it. He was silent for a bit, then said to me, "This is your aunt Birdy." He staggered back and indicated the other cigarette-stained walls, where three more photographs were pinned the same way. "All the pictures are of my Birdy. I loved her 'cause she was a grand person. Miss her like I got a chunk punched outta me. I miss her, Penrod." He scrubbed at the white stubble on his cheeks. "But . . . but, that's my affair. That's my problem. When ya choose to love somebody, ya choose the good and the bad. It was my shitty luck she got killed in an accident, but it ain't for nobody to take away my misery. Y'understand? It's mine. I earned it. If ya get into my head and make me better, you're a thief."

I nodded and studied the water blemishes on the walls and ceiling. Beside my feet, issues of the *Havre de Grace Morning Document* were scattered about, discarded in strange triangles and diamond shapes, brown with oldness. "Is it gonna go away?"

"Yeah," he said. "Yeah, sadness eventually will. It always does, even if we don't want it to." Hewitt leaned forward. With calloused fingers, he held my chin so that

I was looking right at him. "Don't ya worry no more. Don't ya worry, 'cause it'll soak from yer system fairly quick."

Closing my eyes, I tried to feel it doing that, but I couldn't.

"Time," Hewitt mumbled, a funny look settling into his bloodshot eyes, "a few hours or a few days. Now, go on to school. You'll need to be smart for what ya got coming."

Chapter Eleven

I raced up Market Street, veered, and headed straight along Congress Avenue. My book bag joggled and jumped, biting into my back. Still, I got to school before the bell rang. Panting and sweating, I plodded into algebra and yanked off my coat while classmates watched me.

About the time Ms. Lang usually struts in using her evil glare on everyone, a substitute teacher passed through the door. Long, curly hair stood up on his head, while his knees jutted inward when he walked. Dumping a load of papers and books on the big wooden desk up front, he told us that Ms. Lang had fainted from exhaustion the previous afternoon. She was recovering at home in bed, which was a funny thing for me to hear since I remembered her wondering, a week before, what would happen if she faked a collapse.

He said, "If you want to send her a get-well card, drop it by the math office."

I would've laughed but felt too depressed.

Later, in history, I watched Daisy rattle off answers about World War II, but I couldn't solve any questions myself. At lunch, I studied her movements and wanted to place a cheek against her delicate brown skin and feel the smooth softness, the hope. After that, school dwindled to an end, and at 2:15, I unloaded books into my locker. Closing it, I turned to find Hurlee standing behind me.

"Hey, Hurlee, what up?"

He slammed a fist into my unfisted hand. "What up with you, Penn?"

"Nothing . . . I guess."

"Dude," he said, a curious look on his face, "you down? That girl dump you?"

"Naw, none of it." I pointed at the top of Hurlee's hand, where he'd adhered a fake tattoo of a fanged snake crawling through the eye sockets of a skull. "I like that."

"Long as I don't take a shower or sweat, it'll look good. Ya going on yer paper route today?"

"Every day except Saturdays."

"Gonna pass by the Citgo?"

"Maybe."

"Visit, man."

I nodded.

I met Daisy out by the buses, and, holding hands, we walked over to the Burger King, where we bought sodas and called to Matty, who was pressing burgers flat on the flamer. Seeing us, he waved his spatula. After we left, I asked Daisy if she wanted to see something neat about Havre de Grace.

"Of course."

I turned and headed north, passing into the poor section of town. Ugly, wilting homes and apartments sprouted up, grocery bags swirling against their steps and in the nooks and corners of their foundations. Old American cars with soft tires were parked on packed-dirt front yards. Pit bulls barked from different, grimy windows, their noses making smear-marks on the glass. Stopping beside a stolen grocery cart, I pointed along a block of wrecked houses.

"That's where my father grew up."

"That house?"

"He hated it."

"It looks awful."

"His momma left his father when Dad was young, so it wasn't kept up."

She stared at the lumpy white building so long I had to pull her hand and lead her under the sooty girders of the train bridge, where a million pigeons swallowed and cooed and released poop like a shower of raindrops. On the other side, we turned and headed toward the Susquehanna River.

North of town, a stone's throw from the big Route 40 Bridge, we entered an old shore-side park where a portion of a canal named the Tidewater and Susquehanna had passed on its way into Havre de Grace. Crossing a soggy lawn, we stopped at an old-fashioned wooden fence. Together, we leaned against it, peering into a passageway of water.

I asked, "You know what a canal is?"

"Since I was three."

"This one used to end in town, but most of it's been filled in."

"Who built it?"

"Don't know. There's more upriver, but just pieces. It used to go to Pennsylvania."

The wind blew, and waves splashed the nearby shore, rippling marsh grasses. Farther out, surf burst against the cement pilings of the Route 40 Bridge. We dropped our heads back and looked into the sky above the silver girders. "Daisy," I said, "you think people can do impossible things?"

"Like what?"

I raised my shoulders. "Like, I don't know, maybe move things around with their thoughts?"

She continued staring at the sky. "No."

"Why not?"

"How would a brain learn to do that?"

"Evolution?"

"How many animals have developed telepathy? It doesn't happen."

I lowered my gaze. "How about people who can read thoughts?"

"Fake."

"Fake?"

"Of course. It's all fake." A playful smile on her face, she adjusted her coat.

I peered down into the still, black waters of the old canal, red and yellow leaves floating on the surface. "What if you had a friend who could?"

"I'd tell them to see a doctor."

I stuttered, "Y-y-y-ou would?"

"I wouldn't believe them, is all. What's the matter, Penn, you think you're psychic or something?"

"No. I . . . I was just curious. I'm reading a book, and I was wondering." I turned away and leaned hard against the fence. When I spoke again, I tried to sound like I'd become interested in a different subject. "This canal was supposed to make Havre de Grace one of the richest towns in America."

"Wasn't very successful, huh?"

"It stunk."

Daisy reached over and fiddled with my nearest hand. She lifted it and investigated the hangnail flaps on each finger. "I started writing a poem about Havre de Grace."

"Yeah?" I said, but I didn't want to hear it. "You think it's amazing that people dug this all the way to Pennsylvania?"

"If you consider how they were made, canals seem unbelievable."

I thought they seemed that way too, but, since we were standing right there, they obviously weren't. That's why Pygmy Syndrome could be real, I told myself. If people could dig a river to Pennsylvania, I might be able to hear into people's heads. "We need to go get my newspapers."

"Okay then," she said, sliding off the rail.

We walked south to the *Havre de Grace Morning Document* offices, where I hauled my bundle around a corner so as to shield us from wind gusts.

In the shut-down doorway of a bank building, I wrapped papers while Daisy leaned against the wall. I stopped. "When you lived in San Francisco, were you ever scared of earthquakes?"

"I didn't consider them too much."

"You weren't scared that San Francisco might fall into the ocean?"

She picked up a paper and twisted it like a telescope. She put it to an eye. "Penn, it's not true. It won't sink. And if it did, what could I have done to stop it?"

"Move away before it happened."

"My dad was assigned there. I couldn't move." She adjusted against the wall. "Anyway, Penn, where'd you hear San Francisco was going to sink?"

"My dad."

"I hate to tell you, but he's wrong."

I wasn't so surprised by that news and kept working.

Overhead, struggling seagulls flapped madly, dropping and rising in the sky like deflected bullets. Trees tilted hard, as if they might topple. Due to how the wind howled, the low rumble of a tugboat carried up and through the streets, its engine trembling loose windowpanes.

We started off, and as we went, we discussed natural disasters, one of my favorite subjects. Stopping to throw, I told her how when I was a kid, Matty and I had been in a weather-related incident. "It was a thunderstorm that swamped our rowboat off Concord Point. I mean, there were like six-foot waves out there, which isn't humongous or anything, but they're pretty big when you're in a dinghy, that's for sure."

Daisy said, "What did you do?"

"We held to the boat and floated in life preservers till a fisherman got us."

She seemed impressed. "When my father was little, he was in four typhoons."

"In a dinghy?"

"No, Penn, in the Philippines."

That seemed less amazing, but I asked, "So, what exactly is a typhoon?"

"It's a hurricane. He was also in four earthquakes."

"And he was okay?"

"Yeah, he's pretty tough." Her teeth started to chatter. I unzipped my coat. "You wanna wear this?"

"You'll get cold, Penn."

"Naw, I'm fine. Swaynes are used to Havre de Grace weather." I gave her my coat and tossed another paper. A gust carried it sideways into a hedge. "Hold on." I ran across the yard, fetched the thing, and placed it on the front door mat. Jogging back, I felt dizzy with love. "You missed the enormous blizzard we had here a few years back. Over three feet of snow fell. Roofs were collapsing all over the place. Grocery stores ran out of food completely. I'm not kidding."

"Listen to this. When we were on vacation in the High Sierras two years ago, we had five feet of snow in two days."

"Five feet!" I jammed my hands deep into my pockets. "I can't even imagine."

"We had to stay an extra three days skiing."

"I'm surprised you're still not stuck."

She laughed and looped her hand in my arm, which was a wonderful feeling. We delivered the rest of my papers and kept walking that way till near five o'clock, when we came to the gates of the Water's Edge condominium complex. I took the opportunity to kiss her and, backing away, shivered.

She handed over my coat. "Now you're cold."

"I'm fine," I said, but I wasn't actually. It wasn't that I was chilly, though. I was growing anxious that I might not see her for a while. "I . . . I won't be in school tomorrow."

"Are you guys going away for Thanksgiving?"

"Got a doctor's appointment in the morning, is all." I swallowed. "You guys going somewhere?"

"Nope. We never do." She squeezed my hand. "Call, okay?"

"I will." I left, and, feeling sorry for myself, plotted a course over to Millard Tydings Park, where I stood sadly as daylight dimmed. Blocking out the leafless trees with a hand, I tried to imagine that it was July and I was hot and sweaty-feeling. It was impossible to pretend something so contrary, though. The howling breeze was beating against me and whipping up the Chesapeake Bay, forcing swamp reeds flat so that from a distance they reminded me of spilled toothpicks. All around, the hinged flaps of garbage cans screeched back and forth. Way out into the bay, a barge ground southward.

I studied the big platform and the tug that was pushing it and wondered why anyone was trying to go somewhere in that sort of heavy weather. The tug's running lights disappeared and reappeared from behind breaking waves. Retracting my hands into the sleeves of my coat, I thought about the old days, when wooden ships and oyster boats called skipjacks used sails to travel. I wondered if Pygmy Syndrome had existed back then. I figured it had to.

Amidst a dustup of sand and tiny pebbles, fat, widespread drops of rain smacked the ground around my feet. I didn't budge. I was mesmerized, feeling low and watching that barge struggle. It made me think I wasn't struggling enough, that even if I didn't have Pygmy Syndrome, even if I was just a loser with a problem, struggling might be the answer. Maybe I could force my way through to a clear spot or better weather.

Chapter Twelve

The next morning, after my shower, I found two new whiskers on my chin. Leaning close to the mirror, I pulled on both so that the skin stretched to tiny points.

As I came out of the bathroom, steam churned about me like turning wheels. With a toe, I swung the door to my room closed and sat like a famous sculpture atop Granddad Penrod's bed. I thought about the marks I'd scratched into the frame, the way I'd used them to count normal days, and I hoped to cut thousands more.

I chewed at a fingernail and flicked it away.

Lightning flashed outside, turning my room white and bright. Rain hit the window and the buckets and pans across my floor filled. I got up and pulled on some clothes, clomped downstairs, and passed through our sparsely furnished dining room. I stopped at the kitchen door. My father looked at me from the breakfast table. I could tell from his clothes that he wasn't going to work.

"What's wrong?" I asked.

"Staying home."

Matty and him were playing tabletop football, swatting a triangular fold of paper with their fingertips.

"He's losing," Matty told me.

Dad ran a palm over the tiny bristles on his cue-ball head. "Your momma's schedule is too tight to take you to the doctor's today, so I volunteered. For my money, you're gonna be okay. I decided that last night. I got a good feeling about it."

Momma said, "Stew, you need to take a wait-and-see attitude."

Dad winked at me before bumping the triangular football to the floor.

Matty fetched it. "You always hit too hard."

"He always has," I said.

Matty reached over and stroked my father's hand like it was a baby rabbit. "I think his fingers are too strong from lifting bricks."

"It ain't the bricks." Dad laughed. "It's that I ain't good at doing delicate things."

I got some cereal and slurped down breakfast as they played their game and Momma watched me. When I was done, I dumped the dish into the sink and went up to the bathroom.

I was double-checking my new whiskers when Momma left for work. I yelled goodbye to her while I sat on the toilet with my toothbrush dangling from my mouth.

"I'll call!" she hollered up the stairwell.

"Okay," I said back. In a hand, I held one of those concave mirrors that magnifies facial pores and zits. I finished, put away the mirror, and wandered into my room. Then, uneasy, I went back out to the stairs.

Dad was sitting near the bottom, his back to me. "You ready?"

I tried to seem removed from the situation. "I honestly don't think I need to go. That's what I think."

"Yeah, I understand."

I rubbed an itch. "So . . . ?"

"You gotta. I'm sorry."

"What if I won't?"

"You got no choice."

"Dad, turn around and look. You can tell I'm fine?"

137

"It ain't something for me to judge. But, yeah, I think you might be."

My father sat in the lounge while I skulked down a long hall to the consultation room. I was following Dr. Fjord, his narrow, shovel-shaped shoulder blades bobbing beneath a dress shirt that didn't have a single wrinkle, as if the cleaner had used glue instead of starch. He held the door open for me, and I walked in. Nervous, I stood by a giant desk and looked out at a black leather couch and two matching chairs. Except for about ten diplomas, there wasn't anything decorating the walls.

"Where do I sit?" I asked.

"Where do you want to sit?" Dr. Fjord replied, his whitish hair brushed to perfection, so that it rolled in a soft wave above his forehead. On his pale face, the humongous, dark rims of his tortoise-shell glasses created the look of head lamps.

"Well, I don't wanna take your chair, is all."

"You won't. I'm going to sit behind my desk, so feel free to locate yourself anywhere."

"Except behind your desk," I said, trying to show him that, given the choice to sit anywhere, I could've picked that seat, too. "See what I mean?"

"No, Penrod," Dr. Fjord answered as he settled himself and began scribbling in a pad.

Uneasy, I chose a chair that squished down so deep it was embarrassing. I got up and switched, but the new one did the same thing.

"Penrod," Dr. Fjord announced before I could move to the couch, "what can I do for you?"

"Nothing," I answered.

"Nothing?"

"No, sir. Not really. I feel pretty fine."

A smirk stretched across his face.

"What?"

"Just observing."

We stared at each other for a good amount of time, and eventually, just to hear some noise, I said, "Sir, aren't fjords mountains or hills or something like that?"

"No, Penrod, they're inlets of ocean water surrounded by steep cliffs. They were created by glaciation, or so geologists have surmised."

"Are they mostly in Norway or . . . or around that part of the world?"

"Yes. As a matter of fact, I'm of Norwegian descent." He dropped his gaze and wrote on his paper. After dotting an *i* like he was signing the Declaration of Independence, he said, "Enough about me, Penrod. What about you?"

"I don't know where most of my ancestors are from."

"Nevertheless, your family name is very well known in town."

"In town, Swaynes are known, yes, sir."

Dr. Fjord twisted his golden bracelet around his wrist. "And might I ask your family's reputation? Is it good? Is it bad?"

I shrugged. "It's not the greatest."

"Why is that?"

"Because we do stupid things."

"Do you have any mental illness in your family? Might that be a part of it?"

"No."

"But your family still, as you say, does stupid things?"

"I guess."

"Does that bother you?"

"That we suck?"

"That you have a bad reputation."

"Sometimes it does. But it's not the worst in town, and my momma's family's is good."

Dr. Fjord wrote again.

"Isn't that normal?" I asked, trying to understand why he was taking notes.

"What, Penrod?"

"To be slightly bothered by a bad reputation."

"Yes, to a small degree. The reputation of the father is passed to the son."

"That's what I mean. It's ordinary."

Dr. Fjord ignored me. "So, Penrod, in the conversation my receptionist had with your mother, she wrote that you are . . . how do I say this delicately . . . hearing voices?" He inspected a different page in his pad. "She wrote that you've been acting very unusual and that these voices caused you to have an incident at school." He leaned back. He waved his hands. "These are just conversation starters, Penrod. Do you have a comment?"

I waited. "No, sir, I don't have a comment."

Dr. Fjord shifted and sat forward. "Tell me about these voices."

"I can't."

His fingers tapped against his desktop. "Did they ask you not to talk to me?"

"No, sir."

"Do you hear voices, Penrod?"

I stared at him. I ran my hands up and down my arms and considered telling him that my mother didn't know what she was talking about. But I didn't want to get her in trouble at her work, since part of her job was diagnosing mental illnesses. It seemed like a long time before I spoke. "I told her I hear voices, yeah."

"You don't, though?"

"I made it up."

141

"Why?"

I felt so puny in his sinky chair that I sat forward and mostly held myself up with my legs. "I . . . I don't know."

Smirking the way he had before, Dr. Fjord motioned for me to scoot back. "Relax, Penrod. I'm not accusing you of anything. I'm trying to help. Sit back and relax."

I shook my head. "I can't relax when I sit back. I sink in the chair."

He wrote something down.

"What?" My thighs began to tremble. "Why're you writing that? I sink in the chair. That's all."

Dr. Fjord held his pen above the page of his notebook. "Why are you so jumpy, Penrod?"

"Because I'm not crazy. That's why."

"Penrod, I would never call you crazy. But you do hear voices, don't you? You weren't lying to your mother, were you?"

I refused to talk.

"Let me help you, Penrod. Can't you see that I want to?"

I cocked my head and watched a spot on the carpet between my shoes, where shadows crisscrossed like an X. I didn't trust him. "Look, sir, see, I don't need your help because I know what I got. Okay? But if I told you, you'd think it was a joke. It even sounds stupid to me."

"Why?"

"It just does."

"Tell me."

I didn't.

"You can trust me, Penrod." Dr. Fjord's glasses made him look like a bandit. "I care."

"I'm . . . I'm supposed to keep it a secret."

"So the voices did tell you not to speak to anyone?"

"No."

"Trust me. Talk to me, Penrod. I will listen."

For some reason, I suddenly noticed the clammy nature of his soapy, white face and nearly gagged. I couldn't imagine what it would feel like to always sweat above the lip. Restless, I scooted forward even more, jabbing my elbows onto my quivering knees. For a few silent minutes, he watched me, then my lip suddenly twitched like my history teacher's. Nervous that it would again, I clamped a finger to it, which caused my legs to relax and sent me sinking into the chair. From that position, it was nearly useless fighting. After another silent minute, I gave up. "Dr. Fjord, here's the stupid thing, okay. I can hear people's thoughts. I try not to listen, but I can. Doesn't that sound dumb? It does to me, too, but it's true."

Dr. Fjord entwined his clean fingers. "Do you hear my thoughts right now?"

"No, sir. It only happens sometimes. But it's been happening more."

"Really."

"Yeah. My uncle Hewitt says it'll even get worse."

"Your uncle Hewitt? Who is he?"

I paused. "The old Havre de Grace police chief."

"He informed you that you're hearing people's thoughts?"

I sat quietly before answering, "I guess, yeah. See, a few weeks ago, I saw him down at the Canvasback Café, and he recognized right away what was happening to me. Then after my problem at school, he came to my house."

"Might I ask what problem?"

"After I fell in class."

"Ah, your collapse." Dr. Fjord picked up his pen and wrote a long note. Finished, he brushed something from his shiny desktop. "And where have I heard the name Hewitt?"

"Like I said, he was the police chief."

Dr. Fjord grinned. "Hewitt Swayne. Correct?"

The skin on my face burned hot.

Sticking the side of his pen to his lips, Dr. Fjord jutted out his jaw and thought. He tapped his foot on the floor about a thousand times. "Well, Penrod, your case is certainly unique. It's certainly very complex and multilayered."

144

"I don't have a case. It's not a case if it's real, and it's real."

"I'm sure you think it is."

"It is."

Dr. Fjord removed his glasses and opened a desk drawer. He pulled out a little cloth and he cleaned the lenses, then checked them and wiped some more. Folding the cloth, he rested it back in the drawer. He slid the glasses on and said, "Penrod, did I tell you that I might write a book about mental illness? Did I tell you that I know the coloration and the feel of psychological problems? I have dealt with my fair share of patients. I know that you don't hear people's thoughts, Penrod, and I know that this Hewitt character probably has some sort of alcohol-induced psychosis. I . . ."

"What's *psychosis* mean?"

"It means that he has lost touch with reality."

"He could tell you what's going on in your head."

"I'm sure he could." Dr. Fjord laughed. "Penn, I'm going to need to talk to your parents."

"They aren't here. Just my dad is."

"That'll do." He stood. "Relax, Penrod. I'll be back in a moment."

He left, and, for a second, I did relax. I just sat there, wondering what was going to happen. Then I got to imagining what Dr. Fjord was going to tell my father, and I panicked. I jumped from the sinky chair and rushed down the hallway. At the door to the lounge, I slipped around tall Dr. Fjord and nearly ran into my dad, who was rising from off a sofa. "Dad?" I said. "Dad, he's going to tell you I'm crazy, but I'm not."

My father glanced from me to him and back, devastation reflected in his slump, in the way he hung his head, in his loud breathing.

"I don't tell people they're crazy," Dr. Fjord assured us both.

I said, "He thinks he knows it all, but he doesn't, and I can show you. If you come with me, I can show you that he doesn't know everything."

To shush me, my father raised a finger to his lips. "Hold on a second. Hold on, Penn." He blinked at Dr. Fjord. "Doctor, were you gonna give me some information I oughta hear?"

"Dad," I broke in again, "Dad, what I'm telling you is that I can prove he doesn't know what he's talking about. Come with me, and I can prove it. If you still think I'm crazy, you can bring me back. I promise I'll come."

"Mr. Swayne, I wouldn't recommend doing that."

I said, "You gotta trust me instead of him."

Dad shook his head. He turned back to Dr. Fjord. "Dr. Fjord, you think he's got a problem, don't you? Is that what you think?"

"Mr. Swayne, it is my professional opinion that he does. I think that he could be extremely ill."

My father trembled.

"I can prove I'm okay," I told him, yanking on the sleeve of his shirt.

"Mr. Swayne?" Dr. Fjord said sternly.

Dad took another rattling breath. He turned away, stepped to the sofa, and sat hard. "Doctor, before I hear you out, I gotta give the nod to my boy. No disrespect, you understand? But I gotta let him show me what he wants before I hear you out."

The doctor's face grew cross. "Mr. Swayne, it is more than likely Penrod needs immediate help. He needs tests. Doubtless we should image his brain, check for anything unusual, get him on medication. *Crazy* is not a word I like, but maybe it's one that a man like you understands? Your son could very well be—"

Dad cut him off. "Dr. Fjord, if I don't buy what he's showing me, I'll come back. I'll come back this morning even."

"Mr. Swayne, if you return later, I might not have the time to deal with your son's issues."

"You mean to tell me, he needs immediate help, but if we come back in an hour, he won't get it?"

"Yes," Dr. Fjord replied.

Lines like tarantula legs formed above my father's

brow. He stood again. "Well, you're gonna have to learn to be a little flexible since your job is tinkering with lives and futures, 'cause I can't toss my boy to the wolves if he's saying he can prove that he ain't got an issue. I won't do that."

"I could call the Department of Social Services. I could keep him here."

Dad said, "Go ahead."

The doctor closed his pad. "When you come back, you'll have to wait till my appointment schedule clears."

Dad reached for his coat. "That's fine. I took the day off."

In the truck, Dad hunched over the steering wheel with vacant eyes. He rubbed his chin and tugged on an ear that sort of folds at the top. He didn't start the engine. Instead, he shook his head and leaned and swatted the dash with an iron hard palm.

"I'm normal," I promised.

"A professional doesn't think so."

I tried to put some strength into my voice. "I said I was gonna show you, and I will."

He turned the key and got the engine roaring. "This town. First Matty, now you. This sorry place is trying to destroy us." He rolled down the window and spit. "Where we going?"

"To Uncle Hewitt's."

"Oh . . . great." Dad put the truck into gear, and we began to roll. Outside, plastic trash can lids blew across the streets, while birds hung to branches and phone lines with their feathers bushed out for warmth. Roads were flooding, but my father didn't care. His tires sent small waves crashing into the curbs like we were in a speedboat.

In front of Uncle Hewitt's, we didn't get out right off. In the driver seat, Dad dabbed at his face, twisted, and said that he loved me and always would. Nothing could change that, not even a mental condition. Finished making promises, he opened his door and we rushed through the rain and hustled up the rotten steps. We stood on Hewitt's front porch, and the boards beneath our feet quavered like California, like they might fall away into the bay. Nervous, I knocked and waited. Time passed, and I hammered harder, before pushing at the door. It opened slowly.

"Uncle Hewitt!" I hollered. "Uncle Hewitt! It's Penn!"

He called. "Yeah, what?"

"Can I come in?"

"Why not!"

I stepped into the smelly hallway.

"In the kitchen, Penrod."

We went through the dining room, where the table was stacked with bundles of old newspapers. Similar to the living room, all four walls had a photo of Birdy tacked right in the middle, reminding me of an eviction notice I'd seen on a relative's apartment door.

At the sink, Uncle Hewitt stood washing dishes, suds spilling over, wetting up the checkered linoleum floor with its low spot in the center that filled like an ant's swimming pool. He said, "Ya gonna come by every morning now, Penrod?"

"No."

"What'chu want today?" He nodded at my father, who appeared dazed.

"Uncle Hewitt, you aren't listening to our thoughts?"

He shrugged. "Could if I wanted, but I'm working to keep my brain away. I'm working not to hear. I got a low tolerance for people's problems sometimes."

"You need to stop and hear us now, okay, Uncle Hewitt? You need to show my dad that you can hear into people's heads, or they might commit me to an insane asylum."

My father cleared his throat. "Penn, sweetie, maybe we should just get on outta here? Maybe we oughta leave Uncle Hewitt to his chores and head back to Dr. Ford's. . . ."

Uncle Hewitt interrupted. "Your boy don't need a doctor, Stewart. He don't."

Dad scowled. "Hewitt, I know you're trying to—"

"Stewart, Penrod ain't mentally ill. I promise. Sure, he's hearing voices in his head, which sounds sick, it's true, but he ain't. He's got himself Pygmy Syndrome, like I got at his age." Uncle Hewitt lifted his wrinkled fingers from the suds and scratched in his beard. "The short of it is that he can read minds, and maybe a lot more—I can't tell. But he ain't crazy at all."

"Uncle—"

"Uncle nothing. You're thinking that ya wanna get outta here and go back to some doctor's office, that ya shoulda listened to some quack instead of Penrod. Well, you're wrong. Ya were smart to come here. Fact is, I know every thought you're having. I know, 'cause it's like they're getting broadcast in my head. It's possible, Stewart. It is."

Dad supported his body against the doorframe.

"Ya take all the time ya need to figure it out. I wasn't trying to make him hide it from ya, either. I was gonna tell ya and Belinda, but I was gonna do it my own way. Thing is, ya can't let any doctor tinker with Penrod. Penrod don't need to be drugged or put in some hospital. Ya wanna lose the boy ya know, ya go on and let 'em treat him. Hospitals and medicine're misery. Let him be."

My father gripped the doorframe, and his callused, arthritic fingers squeezed like clamps, turning scarlet. Finally he said, "What's going on here?"

"Wish I could explain it," Uncle Hewitt told him sympathetically. "Wish I could."

Chapter Thirteen

Standing in Uncle Hewitt's kitchen, the floorboards groaning beneath his feet, Dad shook his head. He said to Uncle Hewitt, "I wasn't thinking about Penn's situation. I was thinking of football."

Uncle Hewitt pointed at him. "You was just trying to think of football, but you couldn't do it."

Dad swallowed and seemed a little confused. He thought for a few long seconds. "Okay, now I'm thinking of a number. What is it?"

"Forty-two."

"Eleven."

Uncle Hewitt appeared unconcerned.

But his miss made me shiver. I wanted him to be right all the time, but he hadn't been, and whenever he was wrong, my confidence in Pygmies began to fade, and I became less and less convinced that he could read thoughts at all.

Dad said, "I'm thinking of a place."

"Sacramento."

"God, no! See, Uncle Hewitt, you can't read minds a bit. It was Scranton . . . Scranton, Pennsylvania."

"Whatever—they sound alike."

Dad shuffled into Uncle Hewitt's dirty dining room. Arms straight beneath him like two columns, he supported himself over the messy table, stacks of newspapers arranged like apartment buildings on a miniature city block. "I'll tell you for sure, Hewitt, I'm no believer. Not at all."

"Stewart," Uncle Hewitt rasped, his shirtsleeves soaked, "don't matter what ya believe or don't believe."

"Yes, it does."

"No, it actually don't. 'Cause, either way, it ain't gonna be easy for Penrod. It ain't. He's got a rough road in front."

My father nodded but kept looking at the table.

"I'm intending to help, Stewart. I promise."

"I know that's what you wanna do, but I don't think you are."

At home that afternoon, me, my father, and Matty, who was off from work, sat at the kitchen table. There was a lineup of empty beer bottles, like smoke stacks, by my dad's elbow. He was good and smashed and looked it. Alcohol had turned his face scarlet. His nose was so red it appeared to have been pressed in a door.

Slurring slightly, he said that Momma was going to think he was dumb as hell for walking out of the psychologist's office. "Thing is, I had to give you a chance, Penn. I couldn't ignore you, 'specially since you seemed to know more than I did. You seemed certain." He recoiled slightly because of the chills. "After all this, I'm at a loss, that's for sure. I'm wiped out."

Matty, who was eating a candy bar, swabbed his messy mouth on a sleeve and asked very seriously, "Why are you wiped out?"

My father shivered. "Let's see, Matty. Hewitt's senile and your brother's ill. That's on top of you having brain damage and this town dragging us downward like we're tied to an anchor. Last of all is that brainy asshole Dr. Ford I got to go back and see with my tail tucked between my legs."

I said, "Dad, his name's Dr. Fjord, like those things on the coast of Norway."

He pointed with the rim of his beer bottle. "I'm talking 'bout that prick you saw this morning."

"Dr. Fjord."

"Yeah, whatever . . . the snob."

Matty touched one of my father's wrists, smearing chocolate on a cuff. "Dad, what's wrong with Uncle Hewitt?"

"Nothing, Matty," he said sharply. "He's senile, is all. It means he's unstable."

"He seemed fine the other night. He didn't seem 'unstabled.'"

Dad laughed. "Did you look at him? He's a drunk. He's dirty. Used to be he was smart. Used to be he'd think somebody hearing voices was strange. Used to be he was clean and people even hoped he'd run for mayor one day. There was a time when Uncle Hewitt wasn't like now."

I whispered, "Maybe he was good at his job 'cause he heard what people were thinking?"

My father bowed his head. "Come on, Penn. You really believe he can read minds?"

"Maybe, yeah."

Dad coughed for a moment, then, grunting, he struggled to rise, his big thighs caught beneath the table. As he stumbled backward, his chair tipped over.

He shook his head. "God Almighty, Penn, I'm sorry. I'm so sorry for acting crummy and hurt by your problems." His mouth twitched open and closed. "It's all just sort of overwhelming. But I love you. Don't forget, no matter how broken you are."

In view of the fact that Matty came with me on my paper route, I got him a Slushee while I was buying myself a Coke. After that, we went to the Rite Aid, where I searched through three different sizes of Whitman's chocolate samplers and decided on a large, plastic-sealed box shaped like a heart. For Thanksgiving, I was going to drop it secretly at Daisy's front door. After situating it in my newspaper bag, Matty and I wandered on through the chilly streets.

Near the decoy museum, Matty said, "Penn?"

"Yeah?"

"Why's it hurt your head if you drink a Slushee fast?"

"I don't know."

"Maybe . . . maybe it freezes your skull and jaw-bone?" He stopped. "You think when I'm done with my Slushee, I can sneak a chocolate from your box? We can arrange it so Daisy won't be able to tell."

"We're not tearing off the wrapper."

"Come on, Penn."

"You aren't getting one," I told him, smiling.

When we got home, I avoided my dad, who'd stopped drinking and was wearing an apron to cook dinner. I went directly upstairs to my room and called Daisy on the phone. "Hey," I said when she answered.

"Hey."

"Was school okay?"

"Lunch was kind of quiet."

I admitted, "Normally, I talk a lot."

"You have a lot to say."

"Nothing important."

She laughed. "Penn, what happened at the doctor's?"

"We didn't go. My appointment got kind of messed up. We gotta do it again next week."

Out my window and across Millard Tydings Park, the night was creeping in amongst weepy tree limbs, staining everything brown, like an old photograph.

I said, "I called to tell you I'm gonna call tomorrow."

"Good."

"I . . . I like hearing your voice."

"I like hearing yours."

Daisy and I said goodbye, and I pressed the *off* button on the phone. I carried it downstairs and dumped it on a table in the living room. Tired, I sat on the sofa above Matty, who rested on the floor watching television.

Every afternoon he wasn't working, he caught reruns of an old detective show.

As usual, I asked, "You like this?"

"I like how he lives in Hawaii and drives a sports car. It makes me feel good." He twisted and peered at me from over a shoulder.

"What? Do I have something on my face?"

"No. I'm just looking at you 'cause you're my brother." Swiveling back, he watched the detective pick a lock and sneak into somebody's fancy cabana house.

In the foyer, the door opened and Momma arrived home.

My father, all nervous, scrambled out of the kitchen and swayed in front of her similar to a crab-pot marker in peaceful water.

Serious, even a little scary, Momma said to him, "Okay, I'm home, Stew. So what was the problem at Dr. Fjord's office?"

He answered, "Nothing too much."

"Can you do better than that? I've been a little anxious."

"It's just, we gotta go back 'cause I took Penn outta there and over to Uncle Hewitt's. I ignored the doctor's advice."

Dad shuffled closer and sat on the second step of our stairwell. He dangled forward over his knees and took a long breath. "The doctor agreed with you. He wants to run tests and thinks Penn could have an issue. But, see, Belinda, Penn was right there, and he argued to me that he wasn't sick and that he could prove it, and . . . and I had to give him that. He was desperate and begging, Belinda. You should've been there. He really believed. So I had to give him a chance."

"No, you didn't," Momma replied.

"You would've, too. He's our boy, is why, and he wanted to go over to Uncle Hewitt's house in order to prove something."

Momma scrutinized me. "Since when do you visit Uncle Hewitt?"

I stood up. "Since lately."

"That doesn't matter," Dad mumbled. "It was a good thing I went. He's got Penn believing in miracles. He's got him thinking they both hear into other peoples' heads."

Momma closed her eyes.

"Belinda, Uncle Hewitt can't read minds. I checked."

Momma hissed, "Stewart, please."

I told her, "It's the truth. I'm not sick. I explained it to Dr. Fjord, and he didn't listen, but you have to. And I'll show you the truth when I can. I promise. I'm not sick."

160

"You're going to show me that you've got extra-sensory perception?" She stared into the cobwebby corners of the ceiling.

"When it's happening, I'll tell you everything you're thinking. You won't believe it."

Tears scuttled from her eyelids and rolled down to her sharp jaw, where they hung like icicles.

"Can we just treat me like I'm normal?"

"Unfortunately, we can't," she said.

Chapter Fourteen

On account of what Momma felt about my mental state, Thanksgiving morning was uncomfortable and tense, not like normal. Momma, who was wearing a striped apron and basting the turkey in the kitchen, watched me whenever I passed, asking, "Are you feeling well?" or "Is everything fine?" or "Do you feel like yourself?"

"Yes," I kept telling her. And it was true. I was feeling perfectly normal and wanted to avoid the whole topic of illness or ESP.

Late in the morning, she stopped what she was doing and explained, "I'm not mad at you—I hope you know."

"I didn't think you were."

She took long draws of wind. "I'm considering telling Uncle Hewitt to stay away. He is not helping the situation."

"He's okay."

"Also, tomorrow I'm scheduling another appointment with Dr. Fjord. I'll clear my schedule and take you myself."

I leaned against the table and felt the smooth top beneath my palms. I could barely stand to hear Dr. Fjord's name. "I already knew you would."

Before midday supper, my father came and stood near me and Matty as we watched football pregame shows. He dusted the edge of the television with his fingertips and played like he was enthralled by an interview with a coach. When it was over, he adjusted and yawned and casually asked me to walk around the yard with him.

Together, we circled the house making small talk, our hands lazy and in our pants pockets to keep warm. Back around by the front door, he stopped and flicked some yellow fallen leaves off a shrub. "Sorry about the way I acted yesterday."

I looked at the tips of my toes. I wanted to say something that would knock him to his knees, something cruel. I was mad at him for drinking and acting as if I was a ruined teenager. "It's all right."

"It's not." He flexed his fingers and gave the front steps a gentle kick. "I'm embarrassed."

I lifted my chin sternly. "Just tell me the truth, Dad. Do you wonder, a little, if maybe Uncle Hewitt's right?"

He laughed. "I wish he was." He kept a grin on his face and unzipped his coat so as to shove wads of his white dress shirt under his elastic pants seam. "I want you to be a healthy boy, believe me, Penn. If that meant you could hear into heads, that's fine by me. But you can't. There ain't any such thing."

I didn't answer that. "Can I go in now?"

"Yeah."

At one o'clock, Thanksgiving dinner commenced, and it was weird. Momma and Dad took the wimpiest bites, as if they had to be cautious about not eating or drinking too much around me, like stuffing themselves might push me off my rocker.

Candles flickered and flamed and melted down. Matty took over and told a lot of Burger King stories without endings, but, for the most part, we shared the awkward quiet of people feeling awkward. Near the end of the meal, Dad must've gotten worn out by the way things were going, because he folded his arms in a knot across his chest and informed us that my momma's parents were eating their turkey dinners alongside the big swimming pool at their Florida retirement home.

"What if somebody splashes their plates?" Matty asked.

Dad said, "If that happens, I hope management buys 'em new dinners."

Momma offered, "Old people don't splash so much, anyway."

Matty looked in my direction.

"I'm with Momma. I don't think old people splash much."

"Do they use diving boards?"

"Course they do, Matty," Dad told him.

"Well, they might splash when they do that."

"They might, yeah."

Before dessert, I circled the table, grabbing up dirty dinner plates and empty serving dishes. I carried the china into the kitchen, where Momma was scrubbing things silently, without music or anyone's help. It was like celebrating Thanksgiving in a funeral parlor. Everyone was being too hushed and respectful so that I was relieved when we left for the Swayne family Thanksgiving party at Hurlee's parents' house.

Shushed, the four of us wandered up Union Avenue. In the distance was the Route 40 Bridge, which I kept my eyes on in order to occupy myself. Right before the train tracks, we hung a left, so that off to the right the rails looped softly southward, lopping off numerous back yards. Of the thirty or so ugly whitewashed homes spread out on both sides of us, not one had a single tree or shrub to ease their hardness. Mid-block, we zigzagged through a forest of chrome-covered chopper motorcycles and rusty autos and arrived at Hurlee's door.

Inside, the place was packed with relatives. From front to back, people I recognized and strangers alike burrowed around each other like a nest of termites. In every room, the air was hot and heavy with body odor and cigarette smoke drifting similar to ribbons of tugboat exhaust. A lot of the old men had tattoos of blurry anchors, battleships, or crosses on their forearms.

Together, me and Matty shoved our way to the back of the house, past aunts and uncles we barely ever saw. As usual, it was like tromping through the rings of a busy circus. In the back room, we stood in front of a sliding glass door for a second, then I hauled it wide and me and Matty stepped out to join the other teenagers. It was a Thanksgiving tradition among the Swayne kids to hang outside playing angry and unhappy about the holiday season.

I nodded to the closest cousins.

"Yo, Penn," one named Maryjo called. Even though she was a year older than me, we'd always been friendly. In the crook of an arm, she carelessly held her snow-suited baby. She came over and gave me an incredibly putrid-smelling hug.

"Good to see ya."

"Yeah," I answered, my face wrinkling uncontrollably.

"Absoluth's got herself a stinky diaper," Maryjo explained.

"I couldn't change a diaper for fifty dollars."

"Could for nothing if you had to. So Hurlee says you been sick."

"Naw. I been feeling crummy but not sick."

"Don't look so bad," she said seriously. "You . . . you got a girlfriend, too, he said."

"Yeah, she's cool. She's real friendly and smart."

"Don't wanna be changing diapers, keep a cap on it."

"I'm gonna."

Absolut cried and Maryjo said, "She's hungry," and went back to where she'd been sitting. I decided to breathe fresh air over where Matty was talking to a younger cousin named Gilroy.

"Hey," I said.

"Yo," Gilroy answered. He lit a cigarette and took such a cool-seeming suck that it was hard to believe he wasn't the star on some cop show.

I asked, "How've you been?"

"Good." Gilroy grinned and offered me a Winston.

I shook my head. "Me and Matty already smoked at home."

Matty said, "No we didn't."

"You didn't," I told him, trying to get him to shut up.

The sliding glass door pulled back and our cousin Bing stepped out. Right off, he headed for Gilroy, and the two slammed chests like football players. After backing off, they performed a real intricate handshake.

Bing said, "Yo, Matty. Yo, Penn."

"Yo, Bing."

"Spot me a smoke, homey," Bing said to Gilroy.

Feeling stupid, I fidgeted alongside Matty while our two cousins talked. For a while I listened, then I went over to where Hurlee sat slouched atop a plastic bucket, talking. "Hey," I said. "Happy Thanksgiving."

He took a puff on a cigar that smelled like cherry pie. "Yo, cuz. What up?"

"Nothing." I pointed at the back of his hand. "Got rid of your tattoo."

"Washed off."

"Too bad."

"Dude," he said, "I got more. 'Sides, I don't care 'bout nothing right now. Drank like two quarts'a malt liquor, man. I'm blitzed as hell."

I held out a hand. "How many fingers am I holding up?"

"Twenty, cuz," he mumbled blearily, pointing at me. "Ya wanna beer? Got two more quarts stashed."

Our cousin Murphy, who was a senior in high school, said, "It ain't beer, Hurlee. Malt liquor's like the finest, best type of beer you can get. It's differnt. Made'a malt, dude, and . . . and, wheat and crap like that. Penn, it's like drinking champagne 'cept it ain't for wussies."

"You had some, too?"

"Finished like three quarts. Don't seem it 'cause I can hold more'an Hurlee."

"Screw you, Murph," Hurlee said, searching about and picking up a small pebble of cement, which he threw at him.

Murphy skittered out of the way.

Hurlee took a drag on his dessert cigar. "Yo, Penn, ya wanna hit on this?"

"Naw, smoked at home, man."

Hurlee smirked at Murphy. "Told ya. He's scared if he smokes he'll get a reaction."

"What type of reaction, dude?" Murphy asked, a huge grin spreading across his face.

Hurlee shouted, "He's worried 'bout venereal disease! He's scared of catching the clap from tobacco!"

"That ain't so bright," Murphy informed me.

The three of us passed around insults for about an hour. Hurlee kept drinking till he turned pale and sweaty, then got up and vomited by the side of the house.

Everybody in the backyard heard him doing it, too, because he sounded like a strange animal.

A few minutes later, Momma came out the sliding glass door. "Hey, Aunt Belinda," Hurlee muttered as he wiped his mouth.

"Happy Thanksgiving, Hurlee," she told him curtly. Scowling at me, she said that she was heading home, that she was tired.

"Since I got something to deliver to Daisy, you mind if I come?"

She shook her head.

Matty was busy playing with Absoluth, so he stayed while me and Momma headed around to the sidewalk. When we were halfway to the corner, a Doritos bag skipped joyfully by like a cartoon dog. We watched it pass, and then Momma started in on the dangers of alcohol. On and on she went, ending a few blocks from our house with how it could very well increase my mental problems.

"If I have 'em."

"If you have them."

"I didn't drink anything, anyway."

"I'm not accusing you, Penn. I'm just informing you."

I swung my head sideways and realized we were in front of Mrs. Mitchell's house. I slowed and wondered how she was doing since the night I'd taken her depression. Her faded flower drapes were pulled closed so that nobody could see in, causing me to speculate that she was feeling bad again.

Then I thought of a way to test the truth about Pygmy Syndrome. Trudging alongside Momma, my pulse started pounding in both wrists, making my hands feel like balloons. When I got to our house, I went straight up to my room, where I got a grip on my fears and took out the heart-shaped Whitman's chocolates box I'd bought for Daisy. I stared at it for a few minutes, then headed down the steps and out through the kitchen. I marched up the block to Mrs. Mitchell's house and rapped on her door.

She opened it, with the chain on, so that I was forced to look at her through a small crack. Even from there, though, I could see that her eyes were bleak and that she was wearing her nightclothes. The top part of her housecoat's collar was stained by something dark, like Pepsi Cola, as if she'd let herself fall back into disrepair or had never come out of it in the first place.

"Mrs. Mitchell?"

Confused, she said, "Penrod?" in her scratchy, old-lady voice.

"Hey . . . ah . . . I was just thinking about you."

"You were?"

"Yeah . . . um, are you sad is what I was worried."

"Am I sad?"

"I was wondering, yeah. I was at home eating Thanksgiving dinner and just got to thinking that your husband died about a year ago and that you might be lonesome 'cause your kids are busy with their own families." I shifted from foot to foot, nervous about what her response would be.

She seemed surprised. "It was kind of you to think about me. It's been lonely, yes."

"Yeah," I agreed. "I thought so. That's why I brought you a box of chocolates."

She smiled.

"I also got some questions for you. Can I come in?"

She shuffled back a few inches from the crack. "No, I'm sorry. But you hear so many things about teenagers these days. I just read a story about a man who was murdered by his son for a drawer full of coins."

Shocked, I said, "God, Mrs. Mitchell, I wouldn't murder you." Because of the roundabout way she was accusing me of plotting homicide, I wished I wasn't giving her the box of chocolates. "I just wanted to know, do you miss your husband?"

"Very much," she muttered. "We used to do nearly everything together. Are you old enough to remember our scooters? We rode them around town every afternoon."

"I always liked the way you guys looked."

"Me too, very much."

I asked, "Can't you call your kids?"

She appeared ashamed. "Like you said, Penrod, they've got their own families."

"Are you depressed?"

"I suppose I don't feel wonderful."

"You don't ever wanna die do you?"

She gave my question some consideration. "I don't understand why I'm still here, not at my age. I simply don't understand my purpose anymore, if that's what you mean."

"Mrs. Mitchell," I said, "people don't have purposes. We just are."

She touched her hand on a cross hanging about her neck. "Believe me, Penrod, if you look hard enough, there's a purpose for everything and everyone."

I didn't know how to reply, so I handed the box of chocolates through the crack in her door. "Mrs. Mitchell, I got to know, did you feel a little better a few days ago? Were you feeling sad and just felt a little better suddenly?"

She examined my gift, making sure that the wrapper was sealed. "How many days ago?"

"On Tuesday."

She tilted her head. "Yes, come to think of it, I

173

suppose I felt a little better. Then again, the holidays are approaching, and any optimism gets quickly winnowed away by how much I miss Mr. Mitchell. He loved this time of year. I'm sure you don't remember his sense of humor, but . . ."

I cared about what she said, but I was too relieved and excited to hear her very well. I mean, she'd felt better a few days before, which fit perfectly into my calendar. "So," I interrupted, "you just felt better for no reason?"

"Penrod, there're reasons for everything."

I grinned. "Well . . . I . . . I hope the chocolates make you feel even more better. That's their reason for being."

"It was kind of you to think of me."

"I know," I answered, stepping backward, like a car angling in reverse out of a driveway. I wanted to shake a fist, to show relief. Not only was it true that I heard voices, but I'd made a difference. I could secretly make people feel better. That was worth the discomfort of hearing thoughts. I had a power that could do some good, and that felt nice.

She leaned forward. "Are you leaving already?"

"I've gotta be at my uncle's house. I just came by to check on you." I stopped. "Do you really think everything has a purpose?"

"Yes, Penrod, I—"

"That's cool," I told her, stumbling down her sidewalk backward. "Thanks. I appreciate it, and don't worry, those chocolates aren't poisoned. The wrapper's not torn even a little." Then I spun about and ran.

Chapter Fifteen

My stomach felt hollow and dimly painful from a combination of worry and relief. I was worried because I imagined Mrs. Mitchell calling the police to investigate the chocolates I'd given her. I was relieved because I had proof that I was a Pygmy and because I had a clear and obvious purpose to my life.

Trains screeched and pounded their way through town and over the Susquehanna River bridges, and I passed quickly along, listening to their steel wheels bump and looking for my uncle. By the *Havre de Grace Morning Document*'s office, I stopped at a payphone and studied it for a second before picking up the receiver and dialing the operator, who I asked to give me the Parra residence on Chesapeake Drive. When the electronic voice read off the digits, I hung up and watched the cord sway in front of the mangled coin box. When it stopped, I lifted the receiver and slipped in some change.

Following a few rings, Daisy's father snatched up the phone. "Hello," he said with a strange, choppy, Spanish-sounding accent.

I replied, "Hello, sir. Ah, is Daisy in?"

"She's eating Thanksgiving dinner, son. Can I help you?"

I wasn't sure. "Well, sir, I . . . do you think I can say something to her real fast?"

There was a moment of silence. "You may do so very quickly," he stated and the phone was put down.

I waited and watched the road for police officers.

"Hello?"

"Hey, Daisy. It's Penn."

"Penn," she said. "Happy Thanksgiving."

"You too."

"Real quick, my parents asked if want you to come for dinner tomorrow night. You think you can?"

"That'd be cool."

"Good."

"Should I . . . ah . . . bring something?"

"Like what?"

"I don't know."

"Just come." She took a deep breath, like she was surrendering. "I should get back to the table. They won't eat unless I'm there. Can you call later?"

"I will," I told her before blurting, "Oh, and I think . . . I think I almost, maybe, love you. Bye." I hung up the phone before she could answer back. I was gutless. I wanted her to love me, but I didn't want to hear if she didn't. I stood there and ached to tell Daisy about Mrs. Mitchell, as if I might never see her again.

I resumed looking for Uncle Hewitt, who I figured was out at a bar for Thanksgiving. I rushed along the sidewalk and went into Sturgeon's. Inside, not including three haggard men, it was empty. Beneath my feet, the tiled floor seemed slick and oiled, as if it was the frozen surface of a lake. An antique, wavy television was bracketed directly above the men's room door. On it, a football game was playing. I went over to the long bar, which was covered in peanut shells. "Is Hewitt Swayne around?"

"Ain't seen him all day," the bartender answered. "Now get on outta here 'fore I lose my liquor license."

Outside, I peered up and down the commercial strip. I went up a block and into the Chug-A-Lug Lounge.

"Ain't seen him," a guy sitting at the bar told me, and ate a soup cracker.

From there, I went to Shingles Café, where a few of my dad's coworkers said that Uncle Hewitt had bought himself a six-pack early in the afternoon.

"You think he went home?"

Across the counter, the bartender snapped a row of false teeth into his mouth. "Think he was gonna go sit by the water. Think that's what he said. Course, he always mumbles, and most of the time it don't mean nothing."

Leaving out the door, I made like a bullet for the bulkhead and started north around the piles of strewn trash and old industrial buildings. Above, the sky collected a few white cloudy patches, and seagulls cut graceful, smooth lines. I circled a broken dock that extended out into the water from Banger's Warehouse. Due to the way the old building pitched, the place resembled a torpedoed ship. From there, I traced the black creosote boards of the bulkhead, slipping and stumbling over bottles and dissolving paper as I went. Alongside me, the choppy Chesapeake Bay slapped waves against the wall, clipping and clopping like horse hooves. I went about a half mile more before I saw Uncle Hewitt, seated on the sinking wall of the Whistle Bottle-Making Company, out of business for forty years. I walked straight to him and stopped about three feet away.

"Hey," he said.

"Hey."

He swayed his unshaved face in my direction. "Penrod, what'cha want?"

"You . . . you can't tell."

"I'm drunk."

I nodded. "Don't want anything, really. It's just, I checked on the lady whose mood I took the other day."

"And?"

"And . . . I guess I really must've done something. She said that she felt better Tuesday, then she'd gotten sad again on account of the holidays and loneliness." I smiled. "I made her better."

Uncle Hewitt slipped a hand into a pocket of his windbreaker. Moving his body this way and that, he fished around for something till he got frustrated and pulled the pocket wide so that he could look in. Behind tissues and cigarette butts, he uncovered a half-flattened pack of generic cigarettes and a bright yellow lighter that appeared out of place in his hands. He lit up his bargain brand smoke and blew out. "Let me see," he said softly. "Let me see now." He considered for a minute and continued. "Penrod, I didn't say nothing the other day, but ya ain't the first to take someone's mood. Were other guys who could. Was a man by the name of Alvin

'Mosquito' Johnston. Was a Pygmy, a leader. Died about sixty-five years back now, but he had the same talent."

I plopped myself into a clump of grass beside Uncle Hewitt's shoes.

He shook his head. "Watch ya don't cut yer rump. Who knows how many bottles been broken out here."

I stood up.

"Take a seat alongside me."

I nodded and leaned against the extinct factory's old walls.

"You're curious about things, huh? Ya don't know and ya don't understand."

"Are you in my head?"

"Yeah," he said. "Sorry, but, yeah, I am."

"That's all right."

Uncle Hewitt grimaced. He lifted one of his crêpe-papery hands, purple veins like loose extension cords, and studied the tip of his smoke as if it was a sparkler. "Where do Pygmies come from, Penrod? I don't know. Nobody really does. We've just been here. I suppose we evolved out of something. I guess we're here 'cause of some evolutionary break, but who can say?"

I pulled my coat tight across my chest. "Do you know a lot of other people who are like us?"

Uncle Hewitt's lips sucked against his teeth, and he

leaned and picked a beer from his almost finished six-pack. Holding it loosely, he ran a thumb across the pull top, then clunked it back into the brown weeds beside his pants cuffs. "Yup. I know a lot, least the ones in America. Had contact with others. Penrod, Pygmies find each other. We know. That's how I knew 'bout ya. When ya get older, as soon as ya pass a Pygmy, you'll turn round and they will, too. That's why there's been a group, a bodiless organization so to speak, for as long as anyone remembers. It's 'cause we always recognize one another. We've come together to lend support and form some rules. We got the oldest club in the world, I bet."

In the quiet after his voice trailed off, I listened to the nice, regular sounds of waves slosh and seagulls squall.

"I can tell ya more, or I can stop."

After a minute, I answered him. "Say more."

He dipped his head and bent forward over his legs. "Being a Pygmy ain't nothing fantastic or mystical, I promise. Often, we suffer from all the secrets we know, and suffering people need friends. Other thing is, our group basically makes sure we all walk the straight and narrow and don't turn to a life of crime. A man with the ability to read minds could do an awful lot of damage, see." He took a puff on his cigarette and allowed the smoke to crawl up from around his tongue like tired, gray moths. "Ya know the Nazis?"

"Yeah."

"Pygmies knew what Hitler was gonna do and tried to stop him, but we couldn't. Ya heard of Napoleon?"

"The French guy?"

"Was a French dictator with a heart like a knife. Ya ever heard the term *Napoleonic complex*?"

"No."

"It's a chip on yer shoulder for being short. Well, Napoleon, by all accounts, had a God-damned boulder on his shoulder. No joke. He was a Pygmy—a king no less, 'fore he was deposed." Uncle Hewitt sat quiet for a few minutes, then dropped his cigarette and blotted it in the shifty soil. He peered over at me in an odd, tough way. "You're strong enough to be a king one day. Ya got it. I can tell and see it right this very minute." Hewitt took a sniff at the salty air and stayed quiet, like he'd fallen off to sleep. The wind adjusted the limp sections of his combed hair.

Feeling numb and cut off from myself and him, I stared at a boat that was straight across the water from us. Bright and sleek, it pumped through the swells, painting white lines with its droning propeller. The land behind it seemed to move the opposite way, like it was on a conveyor belt and slipping toward Pennsylvania at about a half-mile-an-hour. The craft went on by and eventually rounded the point of land where the light-house sits and the bay opens up wider.

Uncle Hewitt appeared to be lost, his face vacant and strange. Then he said, "After this place shut down, me and Birdy used to come out here. That's why I like sitting along the water, 'cause we did it together. I loved that. Heck, I used to work at the Whistle Bottle-Making Company in the summer when I was a boy in high school. Worked the automatic bottle-blowing machine. Pressed out about ten thousand bottles for Patriot soda, which was this gunky, syrupy cherry cola that was a big, big failure. Man, my arms got tired, too. No computers back then. I pulled a lever and squeezed in a bunch of molten glass, got the machine going, the air blasting and pushing the hot glass into molds, and after a few minutes, I had twelve bottles to send on down the line. Was sixteen years old when I started, Penrod. I coulda heard every single one of my coworkers' thoughts, if I'd wanted. I struggled not to, though. I learned to focus so I only heard a few, but it was hard and still is. Had a nice lady Pygmy come visit and ease me into my new situation. I'd work all day, my arms sore and my brain as ripped and tired as you'd ever guess, but I got through, and . . . and you're gonna, too."

I smiled. "Thanks, Uncle Hewitt."

"For what? It's my pleasure, Penrod. Back when I worked here I was a boy, I was older than you, but I was still a boy, young and strong and optimistic. I'd wear leather gloves, and the sweat'd be rolling down my wrists and soaking my rolled-up sleeves at the elbows." He looked over thoughtfully. "Can ya imagine? When I left, I had plans. I did. And I achieved mosta them somehow. Birdy helped me do it. Sure, we didn't have no kids, but that turned out okay. We had each other. And who woulda guessed? After my surprisingly long and successful career in law enforcement, which was due to how I could read the thoughts of crooks, brawlers, and racketeers, I had my sights on being mayor right up to the day your aunt Birdy died." He threw a little rock to the ground. "Christ, that stunk."

"Sorry."

Uncle Hewitt, bent, tugged his windbreaker, and felt around in a pants pocket before locating some salted peanuts. He threw them into his mouth and crunched them with his stained teeth. Swallowing, he pulled his cactus eyebrows into an arch. "But we're all just people, ain't we? We're all struggling to make the best. So I am what I am. I've been worse off. I've been treated by wrong-headed doctors, and there wasn't nothing more horrible, excluding when Birdy left, than that. But . . . but now, here me and ya sit in Havre de Grace, so far removed from other Pygmies and their decisions, it's a dreamy vapor that don't seem like more than a story. See, in a town filled with strange people, empty buildings, and lost jobs, a man can survive in his own little world. He can create his ownself. It's insulated and safe. But I missed out on certain things. I missed out." He looked at me sternly. "I'm trying to make it so ya won't, Penrod. I got a good feeling about ya. You're gonna be fine. You're gonna be the king. That's something that no matter what anyone says ya gotta take into your heart. That's a nice thing for me to let ya in on."

He ate a few more peanuts. "For your own information, soon as I get ya stable and okay with everything, I figure I'll make a phone call up to a man I know in New York, tell him things. After that, others'll probably see to your well-being. Okay? It ain't my job. Nobody'd trust me with it, no how."

I rotated toward him. "Who's the man?"

"Just a guy. He's a scientist fella. He's a Pygmy, too, a good sort who'd talk to your parents, get ya ready for what's ahead." Hewitt scratched his temple. "Seems fantastic, don't it?"

"Yeah. But it's all right."

"Well, it ain't fantastic. It's regular and unspectacular as hell. It's as rusty and hard-knock as a bottle-making factory or fish-freezing plant. It's like being a handicapped person without no one knowing. That's the glamour of it. What I'm saying is, there ain't none. It's glamourless. Ya gotta take it as it comes and hang on like a barnacle."

I arrived home just before dark. My father and Matty sat in the living room watching a football game. Starving, I wandered into the kitchen and found Momma sitting at the table, sipping coffee and staring into shadows.

"You okay?" I asked.

She nodded distantly. "I'm fine. Just sitting here thinking."

I went over to the refrigerator.

"Guess who called a little while ago?"

"Daisy."

"No. It was your other girlfriend, Mrs. Mitchell. She said you brought her some chocolates."

I stopped. "They were for Daisy, but I figured Mrs. Mitchell was lonelier."

"She said you were worried she's depressed."

"I was."

"Why?"

I raised up my shoulders. "Her husband died like a year ago, Momma. That's all."

"I think she felt you were hatching a plot to steal her money."

I laughed. "She's paranoid."

Momma tilted her coffee cup with both hands and drank. "Why, though, Penn? Why Mrs. Mitchell?"

"Why does anyone do anything?"

"That's a cop-out."

I nodded and wondered if I should admit the truth about taking our neighbor's sadness.

"Talk to me, sweetie."

"You want me to?"

"Yes."

I put my hands in my pockets and waited a moment. "I did it 'cause I heard her in the night. I actually did. On Tuesday, after everyone was asleep, her mind told me she was depressed."

I went over to the refrigerator. "Momma, I talked with her soul or something, her spirit, and it told me things about her husband and kids and how she was lonely. I knew all that before she told me this afternoon. By taking her those chocolates, I learned the truth about me."

Momma studied the tabletop like she was trying to read the future in the crumbs scattered on it.

"Why can't you accept that amazing things happen?"

"Because amazing things are one thing; impossible things are another."

"Maybe they never were impossible."

Momma set her mouth sternly. "I know you heard a voice, Penrod. I also accept that you think it was hers. But it wasn't."

"My mind didn't make it up."

"It did."

"It couldn't make up so much. We talked."

"Of course it seemed that way."

Annoyed, I told her, "Hewitt explained how it works for people like me and him. He—"

She spoke over me. "Penn, Hewitt is obviously ill! He's lonely. He drinks far too much. And, he's wrong. He's just wrong."

I stared at her.

"I can't imagine how you feel. I can't pretend to know what it's like to believe something in your heart and have me tell you different. But I am telling you, he's wrong. What you heard wasn't Mrs. Mitchell or her thoughts. What you heard started and ended in your head, with chemicals misfiring and a few imperfect neurological features."

I stayed calm, trying as hard as I could to be sure in myself.

"I'm so sorry," she said.

I didn't answer.

"Are you okay?"

"Yeah."

"I don't want to hurt you, Penn."

"You didn't, 'cause I'm ignoring everything bad you say and holding to what I know."

Chapter Sixteen

The next afternoon, when my paper route was through, I went home, clomped upstairs, and brushed my teeth. Taking a comb, I nervously raked and raked my hair so as to look like a regular, well-mannered teenager. Then I took scissors and trimmed back my longest whiskers. Even though my parents were uncomfortable with the idea, I was going to dinner at Daisy's.

Alongside my father, who'd insisted on escorting me, I walked through the historic and tired streets of Havre de Grace, stopping in Millard Tydings Park. Overhead, in the murky darkness, unseen geese honked past. Without talking, the two of us listened till they were gone. We started stiffly through the patchy grass, ducking beneath and around scratchy branches and small trees on our way back to the street.

"I know how to get there," I told him. "You don't have to make sure."

"Allow me to take a walk with you."

Tramping onto Chesapeake Drive, I could see the Water's Edge condominium complex up ahead. We got to Daisy's building. "Bye," I said.

"Call, and I'll come get you."

"Okay," I told him, but I wasn't going to.

I went up the steps without watching my dad leave, which was funny since the evening reminded me of a story he told about my mother. In our family, it's become like a Greek myth or something.

Twenty-six years back, my momma's parents, the Wallaces, had hosted an introductory dinner for my father. Nervous, my dad had dressed in his best clothes, which weren't much. Also, he'd carried three roses purchased at the National Five and Ten store downtown. All evening, my Wallace grandparents had treated him with polite respect, even when he pulled off the bathroom doorknob and trapped himself inside. As calm as can be, my granddad got him out with some pliers and kept liking him. Excluding getting stuck in the can, I hoped it would be that easy for me. I hoped my relationship with Daisy might end the same way.

I mashed the bell to Daisy's condo and waited square in front of the door. It cracked loose and swung open. Daisy poked her head around, and her prettiness nearly caused me to stop breathing.

"Hey," I said.

"You're all dressed up."

I examined the sleeves of my too-small blue blazer. "It's to make a good impression." I stepped forward and presented her with three roses from the 7-11.

She held them to her nose and sniffed.

I pointed to a little packet that was rubber-banded to their stems. "That keeps 'em fresh in water."

Her hair resembled a black veil atop an exotic Egyptian princess's head. Behind her stood her parents.

Mr. Parra was broad and powerful. He held his spine straight like he had a spike in his rear. He wasn't at all like the Asian butlers on television, the kind who bow a hundred times while they serve tea. His hair was buzz cut, and his face was so sturdy that it could've gotten torpedoed and except for maybe losing a tooth, would still look the same. "I assume this is Penn?" he said to Daisy. Even after talking to him over the phone, his sharp Filipino accent surprised me.

"Hello, sir." I held out my hand.

He crushed my fingers. "Fine to meet you, son."

Daisy's momma's curly hair mirrored the curve of her smile. "I heard a lot about you," she told me in an even thicker accent than her husband's, then proceeded to mash my fingers, too.

"I've heard things about you, ma'am."

Daisy showed her the flowers I'd brought.

"They're beautiful," Mrs. Parra commented.

Inside, their condominium wasn't nearly as Asian as I'd imagined. I'd pictured it full of Filipino things — not that I knew what those were — but it wasn't. It was mostly modern with a few oriental-type knickknacks on the tables, a bowl here, a carved bookend there. I had expected images of Chinese screens painted with colorful, fan-tailed peacocks and bright flowers. I'd expected a dozen or so prints of ladies in kimonos wearing chopsticks dug into their hair buns. Also missing were any dragon images, bonsai trees, or hanging samurai swords. Basically, their house had a standard American feel. As a matter of fact, both of her parents were even wearing sneakers.

The four of us wandered into the living room and stood for a few minutes.

When her parents left us, Daisy asked, "You want to see my room?"

"Sure."

She led me down a hall, and, turning a corner, we stopped short. "There it is."

"We can't go in?"

"I don't think we should."

I nodded and ran my eyes across shelves of books. She owned a ton compared to me. I tried to read a small stack of CDs, but they were too far away. Over them was a map of the world with a face in a corner blowing out air. Tumbled across her desk were schoolbooks and notebooks, all of them opened. Above her bed was a gargantuan black-and-white poster of an older black lady whose facial features were large but pretty, like a lion's.

"Who's that?"

Daisy said, "Maya Angelou. The writer I like."

"Oh."

She led me back down the hallway. In the living room she said, "Let's go stand on the deck. It's the best part of our condo. And it's private."

I took one last whiff of the unique-smelling Asian food her momma was cooking and followed her out.

Their wooden balcony hung high over the muddy shoreline. Even higher, in the indigo sky, seagulls winged. Side by side, me and Daisy brushed shoulders and studied the glittery water. For some reason, being near her eased my worries like a truckload of invisible pillows.

"Does this look like San Francisco Bay?" I asked, almost scatterbrained with joy.

"It's not the same."

"Is the Chesapeake boring to you?"

"It's nice in its own way."

"That's what I think." I twisted to peer through the glass doors of her condo. "I wish we could kiss, except I think your parents might leave the kitchen and see us."

"They might. My father'd get pretty upset, too."

I rotated back around and rested my elbows over the wooden rail. "You wanna hear something funny?"

"What?"

"When my dad first visited my momma's parents, he got stuck in the bathroom 'cause he pulled the doorknob off."

Daisy laughed. "That's mortifying."

"Are your doorknobs on tight?"

"My dad's pretty strong and he's never done it."

I smiled and hesitated before changing my tone and saying, "Daisy?"

"Yeah?"

"Here's a strange question. Do you think general miracles ever happen? Ever?"

"Penn, that's kind of the same question you asked before."

I forced myself to appear nonchalant, which I was getting good at. "I've been thinking about that type of thing lately."

She touched a finger to her bottom lip. "It depends on what you call a miracle."

"I . . . I guess something that seems impossible, like how the universe grew out of an explosion or finding the Loch Ness monster after all these years. I don't know."

She adjusted her hair over an ear. "Well, I don't believe in the Loch Ness monster or Big Foot or any of those things, but I always thought electric eels were kind of that way, and, you know, not so long ago they found that prehistoric fish that was supposed to have died like millions of years ago. Those are small miracles."

"How about big things, too, like voodoo dolls or people who walk across burning coals?"

She breathed softly. "You aren't into voodoo, are you?"

"I'm just asking."

"I think voodoo's creepy."

"Me too. I've been wondering about amazing-seeming things—that's all."

She wrapped one of her hands in mine. "I guess, deep down, I don't believe in the paranormal."

I held her fingers tightly in mine, impressed by how she'd used the word *paranormal*. "Today I was thinking that impossible things are possible or nothing would exist. That's why miracles've gotta happen. You know?"

"I don't actually," she said.

I gazed at her profile. "Scientists can't figure out how life started, but it's here."

"There's an explanation."

"But we don't know it, so it seems like a miracle."

"You can't convince me." She laughed.

I nodded and scooted closer. Level with us, the tops of trees stirred. I told her, "Give me time and maybe I will."

The exotic Asian food I'd smelled cooking turned out to be spaghetti, the Italian kind. During dinner, trying to appear suave, I sucked noodles into my mouth as daintily as I could. I even stretched my neck out like a turtle, hoping I wouldn't splash my good sweater with sauce. Meanwhile, Daisy's parents asked me all sorts of questions. A few times, the choppiness of their accents made me feel like I was getting interrogated, but I could tell it wasn't meant that way.

Later, Daisy and I sat watching television in the sunroom. Seated on a bulging blue couch, our knees almost touched but didn't. The TV blabbed, and Daisy explained how she'd been born in Texas and had moved five times since, whenever her father was transferred to a different Army base. She'd lived in Nevada, Kansas, New Mexico, and California. She'd made dozens of friends and left them all in the dust. Her grandparents and cousins didn't know her and had never crossed the Pacific Ocean to visit. Last but not least, she didn't have any brothers or sisters, which all combined to make her feel unattached and lonely a lot.

I mumbled, "I'd feel that way, too."

She hung her head. "So, what's it like to live in one place your whole life?" The curve of her glasses reflected a stretched picture of my face.

"Like sometimes, here and there, you wanna live somewhere else. I mean, it's nice, too. It's nice to know things about a place. I could lose my sight and still walk around town without bumping things."

"You might get run over."

I grinned. "I forgot about cars."

She said, "I'm sick of being the new person all the time. I really am."

"But you're not so new to me anymore," I said, trying to make her feel wanted. "You're getting less new and more attached every day."

Chapter Seventeen

After breakfast, while my father and Matty were out running errands, Momma surprised me by handing over one of my dad's cement-splotched work coats and saying, "Put it on."

"Why?"

"Because we're leaving." She punched her spindly hands through the channel of her own jacket's sleeves, her engagement ring catching threads near the cuff. She tugged, and the threads broke.

I slipped on my dad's coat and zipped it, which was like wrapping in a smelly, dirt-stiffened towel. Confused,

I followed Momma out the front door and down the steps to the walkway. Silent, we started along Union Avenue. A block up, Momma directed me to turn right on Lafayette Street, which was named after a famous French officer, General Lafayette, who gave Havre de Grace its pretty, European-sounding name on account of it reminding him of a place with that name in France.

"Where we going?" I asked.

"To visit Uncle Hewitt. We need to have a discussion."

I stayed quiet until it seemed that being quiet was somehow evidence that I was ill. "You cold?"

"I'm fine. You?"

"I'm okay."

"Penn, this is going to be a good thing."

"Not for me."

"I promise."

I wouldn't meet her eyes. "You want me to stay away from him—that's all."

"I do, yes. If you were simply depressed, I'd say fine, if he makes you feel better, it's fine. But you aren't depressed. You need others, your family and professionals, to help you discern what's real and what's not, to help you find a balance."

A few blocks ahead, the chilly bay rocked like a shallow bowl of soup. Momma continued by saying, "I believe Uncle Hewitt is psychotic. I do. Without a doubt, he was a wonderful person, an upstanding amazing man in his time, and I have no question that he means well, but I think he's living in a make-believe world and he's drawing you in after him."

I didn't reply and instead noticed the edge of my father's grimy jacket. Wearing such a real thing made it hard to deny that Uncle Hewitt's stories sounded artificial.

Momma reached over and yanked my father's coat across my shoulders. "You smell like cement. I love that."

"I don't."

"It reminds me of being young."

"It reminds me of Dad's work."

She grinned weakly. "I guess it would. It would for you, but for me it brings back the strongest memories of when your father and I were dating and he was attending masonry school. Until then, he'd never smelled of cement."

"That's back when he looked like that fat actor Nick Nolte, right?"

Her grin opened up. "He really did." I could see her calmness and feel her strength. After a minute, her smile faded to a more serious expression. "These last few weeks, I have come to understand what happens to youthful optimism. It goes away." She let her lids shut then drew them back up. "Let's go hear Uncle Hewitt out."

We knocked on his door, but there was no answer. I shoved the barrier open and called to him. There was still nothing. Momma slipped in around me and hollered his name.

We shuffled down the rickety front stairway and stood amongst the weeds of his front yard.

"Do you know where Uncle Hewitt might be?" Momma asked.

"Maybe at a bar? Maybe along the waterfront? You know how he does."

She pulled her hair into a ponytail and used a rubber band from a pocket to keep it in place. "Let's go look."

On the commercial end of Washington Street, we passed a couple packs of unlucky tourists who wandered about confused, like earthquake survivors scrounging around for signs of life in the dusty storefronts. They'd probably planned on visiting the Duck Decoy Museum and wanted to eat breakfast or lunch first. But restaurants, excluding a few bars and the Canvasback Café, didn't open till one o'clock.

Momma went in and out of various drinking holes, searching with a determined silence before, finally, emerging with Uncle Hewitt. I mumbled, "Hey."

He pointed at me and thunked a brown bag down on the sidewalk before rummaging in a frayed shirt pocket for his cigarettes. Shaking one out, he fired up his yellow lighter. "If you wanna talk, Belinda, let's go on back to my house."

"Wherever," she told him.

Ten minutes later, one of Momma's feet went through a stair tread leading up to Uncle Hewitt's front door.

"Sorry," he told her, scratching his head, leaving a rooster comb of hair sticking high. "I gotta fix that."

"If you don't want to get sued, you do."

"Well, I don't wanna."

In his dining room, I noticed details I'd missed before, how beneath each windowsill the wall was decorated with big curls of peeling paint, like the bent necks of swans. I suppose it was water damage, but instead of seeming awful or disgusting, it was pretty, like the wall was wearing a weird, expensive sweater. I touched a graceful coil, causing it to fall and break into pieces.

Momma watched me before saying to Uncle Hewitt, "Haven't visited the house in a long time."

"Place has changed, huh?"

"It's less polished."

The exploded blood vessels in his nose throbbed like tiny neon lights. "So, I know what ya want, Belinda."

"What's that?"

Uncle Hewitt hesitated. "Ya don't believe anything, and ya want me to prove it to ya or quit bugging Penrod."

She put a hand gently on the table and adjusted her weight over one leg. Carefully, as if she was handling somebody with a fragile ego, she said, "Uncle Hewitt, did you just read my mind? Is that how you knew?"

He wavered before chirping, "Yeah."

"How long have you been able to do that?"

"Been forever . . . or since I was Penrod's age."

"You could hear people when you were a teenager?"

"Started exactly the same way as Penrod's, as voices just coming to me outta nowhere. The difference was, it took a few years before I realized what was happening. Before that, I just worried, that's all. Told my dad, and he said it was normal for certain people to hear voices. Turned out, we had an uncle who was the same way. Uncle Cleveland was the fella. Was he ever a midget, or at least bordering on being one. He's why I was mostly calm about my situation."

Momma looked into the kitchen, at the uneven floor and the off-kilter stove. "Did Aunt Birdy know?"

"Oh, yeah. God bless her, she knew. She saw how Pygmy Syndrome gave me a leg up in my job. Gave me a leg up with her, too."

Momma nodded. "Pygmy Syndrome?"

He rubbed a fingernail across a blotchy area of his forehead and gave it a sniff. "That's the name."

"Somebody told it to you?"

"Momma," I interrupted, "there's a whole history that's been going on for like two thousand years. It's intricate."

Uncle Hewitt told her, "Belinda, Pygmies've been here on the earth living parallel to regular humans throughout time. It's just that nobody knew."

"I see," she said. Taking off her coat, she carefully hung it over the back of a chair. Somewhere in the house, a toilet ran and a faucet dripped. Momma seemed to consider what he'd told her. "Who told you about Pygmies? Do you remember?"

"Was Uncle Cleveland at first, then a woman."

"Uncle Cleveland, then a woman. Do you recall her name?"

"Course. Practically speak to her every day. We check in and discuss things. It's nice."

"Does she live around here?"

"Never did. She's from Richmond, but she's old now."

Momma picked up a dust ball and deposited it into an old paint can. "So you guys talk on the phone?"

Hewitt adjusted uncomfortably. "No, Belinda, we don't. We . . . we do it through our brains."

"Your friend, can I contact her? Do you think she'd be bothered by that?"

Uncle Hewitt's reply was quick. "We both would. We keep contact information hidden from the government and all the shrinks who ever ask. Ya psychologists are a buncha blabbermouths and don't believe nothing unless it's as solidly in front of ya as this here table. But I

206

have come to see that things don't have to be absolutely solid and that ya leave people be if they're making it through, no matter the story."

"No matter the story?"

"Yes."

Momma wandered to a wall and examined a photograph of Birdy. After a few minutes, she whispered, "She was a beautiful woman."

Hewitt hacked into a hand then struggled to catch his breath. "Yeah, she was. Had . . . had more than just looks, too. She loved me, and it's love soothes the syndrome like nothing else. Don't know why, but it does."

Momma turned about unhurriedly. "What was it like when she died?"

"Knew you was gonna ask that."

"Did you?"

He tugged on a hairy ear to imply that he'd heard her thoughts. "Saw it flash across your brain." Wobbly, he removed a six-pack from the brown bag he'd carried home and set it on the table. "You wanna know what it was like when Birdy died. Well, it sucked. Thought I was gonna die my ownself from how wounded I was. She . . . she was the only person who ever knew the truth about me. You see what I mean? She knew my secret ability and never questioned me. When she died, it was the worst thing that ever happened. I was cut off. I was set adrift."

Momma studied him, her eyes sheening like pen-lights. "She was the only one who knew you were a Pygmy?"

"Yeah."

"But you knew other Pygmies, right, like your friend from Richmond? If you can talk to them through telepathy, how were you alone?"

Uncle Hewitt lifted his head and looked up his bumpy red nose at her. He was obviously irritated and a little confused. "What I meant is that Birdy knew me better than anyone else. She knew my soul."

"It must've been nice."

"Was."

"But your Pygmy friends can't exactly hear into your soul, huh, even though Penn says he heard our neighbor's talking? You think maybe he really didn't?"

"Some hear."

"Some do?"

"Sometimes . . . maybe. I'd say that it's possible Penn's so strong he does."

"He's that strong?"

"I don't know." He scowled at Momma. "Belinda, just leave him be, that's all."

Momma bit her upper lip. "Hewitt, have any of them visited since Birdy passed? Any of your friends."

"Yeah. Course. More and more come."

"When?"

He said, "Last week. All the time, dozens are joining me for big dinners and drinks. All the time. Sometimes, wish they'd . . . ah . . . leave me be."

Momma cast her eyes about the pigsty in front of her, at the table that was completely covered with newspapers and dust and had only one small cleared spot in front of a chair.

Uncle Hewitt ripped off a beer can and held it to him. He studied the photo my Momma stood beside and smiled back at Aunt Birdy. He said, "Loving her was heaven that turned to hell when she died."

The saddest expression came on Momma's face, and she allowed time before asking, "How'd you know Penn was a Pygmy?"

"'Cause Pygmies know, Belinda. Pygmies can tell other Pygmies. It's a gift. Plus, your boy, he's special, the strongest Pygmy I ever met. He gives off all sorts of signs."

Momma backed up and leaned a shoulder against one of the old walls. As if she was cold, she tucked her hands under her arms.

Opening the beer, Uncle Hewitt gulped at it loudly. Lowering it, he sneered, "Why don't you finish up and ask what ya wanna ask, Belinda, so we can be done with your interrogation."

Momma lowered her chin. "Uncle Hewitt, I can stop right now."

He finished his beer in a few more swallows, and, partially crushing the can between his two hands, he cleared his throat. "Then stop right now."

On our way home, Momma said, "He doesn't have any idea what's real and what's delusion."

I mumbled, "Yes he does." I didn't want to give up being someone who could save people, someone with a great purpose who wasn't sick.

"He didn't read my mind. Not once."

"That's what you say now."

"Okay, Penn, maybe so, but his stories don't hold together."

"They stay together for me."

She slowed and tried to take hold of one of my hands. "He's seen psychiatrists. You heard him. He's been treated, probably hospitalized."

I veered away from her.

"Penn, sweetheart, it's a common story. Birdy kept his two worlds together and functioning, but, when she died, everything fell apart. That type of thing is not uncommon for people suffering mild schizophrenia. They can lead productive lives with the help of a spouse or family member, but take that person away and they crumble." Gently, she pulled silver strands of hair from out of her mouth. "You need to recognize the truth. You need to ignore what you feel and recognize the truth."

On Monday morning, Ms. Lang, who had recovered from her phony fainting spell, was back teaching algebra. With a thump, she took a seat and glowered at us before rising up and taking a stance similar to a tugboat pilot leaning into a gale. Plastering a mean expression on her face, she slogged about popping difficult questions that no one, not even good students, could answer. I felt sorry for her.

At lunch, I took my seat across from Daisy and gave her shy glances. Behind us, a scuffle broke out. Two girls yelled and attacked, clawing and slapping until a load of teachers dragged them apart. Cursing, they both suffered nasty scrapes across their faces. I leaned forward and touched one of Daisy's hands. "I got a question. Am I normal-seeming to you?"

She laughed. "You're definitely not normal. You seemed it at first, but you're not. You think a lot."

I nodded, and, despite the fact she'd given me the wrong answer, a wide wonderful happiness swelled inside of me.

After eating, I sprang along to my next class. At the end of the day, I practically floated Daisy to the Burger

King, where I got us the usual. Holding hands, I led her downtown, past the *Havre de Grace Morning Document* offices and to the bulkhead, where the water sprawled out in front of us like the salt flats in Utah. I lifted one of Daisy's brown hands and kissed each fingertip.

Birds zipped back and forth like weavers knitting something large. The wind blew and Daisy's hair fluttered romantically. I touched it and was amazed by the softness. Feeling good and nostalgic, I told Daisy about the far shore and a town called Port Deposit, which was famous for its granite rock. I said it was where my momma's parents had carried her to swim in a community pool when she was little. Being that it was a longish drive and Havre de Grace was surrounded by water, doing that had always seemed idiotic to me.

"How far away is it?"

"Like twenty-five minutes."

"That's not so bad."

I cranked my head upward and investigated an approaching storm. As always, I knew it would turn before it got to us. "Port Deposit didn't just have a pool. A long time ago, the town had its own canal that was a worse failure than ours."

"Must've been pretty unsuccessful." Daisy laughed.

"Maybe ten people used it." I leaned down and snagged up a flat rock, which I skipped across the water.

Veering ecstatically, like a comedian, I smiled at Daisy. "Once, I saw a show where people put on these pontoon things, like giant, floatable shoes, and they walked across the water. I'd love to do that, would you?"

"Maybe." A line formed on the skin above her nose. "Penn, you seem funny."

"I'm excited is all. I feel good and want to do something unexpected, like walk across the bay. Or, on the cover of a *National Geographic,* I saw a guy paraflying. He had a motor, like a giant house fan, attached to his back, and he actually flew with a parachute out over a desert. He was following a herd of African elephants. I was like . . . wow! You know? It was wild."

My heart racing, I suddenly froze. I found myself studying how her lips melded into the rest of her face in a series of soft curves. For a second or two, I was paralyzed with affection for everything about her, and I knew that despite my issues, our future was brighter than I could ever imagine. Blood rhythmically pinched at the sides of my neck, and she surprised me by saying that she'd love to parasail or walk across the water or do just about anything with me. She just loved being nearby and hearing the strange things I talked about.

"Sometimes, I worry that you'll get tired of me. Well, I don't mean get tired so much as get annoyed. I can be annoying."

Daisy said that she was in love, deep in love.

Feeling romantic and sure of myself, I put a finger against one of her cheeks. I pressed softly against her skin before leaning over and kissing the spot. "Do you remember what I told you over the phone on Thanksgiving, at the end of our conversation? I'm in love, too. I think I love you, too."

She stepped away, creating a distance between us.

"You don't remember?"

Her eyes shifted. "Penn, you're talking to yourself."

I tottered backward. Her lips hadn't been moving. "I'm . . . I'm not talking to myself," I stammered. "I'm just talking too much."

"You're talking a lot."

I nodded. "You didn't say anything about loving me back, did you?"

"I like you. Love is big."

Her comment flattened me like a meteor.

"Penn, I always leave people behind. I've left everybody I was ever friends with. It could happen again, and what if I did love you? It'd be like getting divorced."

"Daisy," I said, feeling confused, "you're meant to be in Havre de Grace. I can tell." Tiny raindrops sputtered from the clouds, speckling our coats and sticking like gnats in our hair. I stayed there for a while, before mumbling, "Let's just go on and deliver my papers."

214

By the time we got to her condominium complex, everything was messed up. She didn't even kiss me. Instead, she said, "While I'm in town, I'll stay with you. Okay?"

But if she knew the truth about me, I didn't think she would.

Chapter Eighteen

Following a long, miserable night of familiar and unfamiliar voices tramping pathways through the leaky walls of my skull, the morning was clear and cold and free of mind-reading or delusions. It was a relief, since Daisy had rejected me and it was, maybe, my final fling with freedom. The next afternoon, I had an appointment to see Dr. Fjord again.

During lunch, Daisy and I looked at each other sadly, awkwardly, and she said, "Penn, I'm sorry about yesterday. I hope I didn't hurt your feelings."

I lied. "You didn't."

"It's the last thing I want to do."

"It's the last thing I want you to do," I said, and it was.

When my paper route was done, my appointment with Dr. Fjord began to loom like an approaching hurricane on a weather map, one that blots out an entire continent. At home, I ransacked the cupboards for a snack while I played messages on the answering machine. The first two were for my mother, the third for my dad. The last was for me.

"Penrod, ah . . . it's me," Uncle Hewitt grumbled. "We gotta get together tonight. I got someone for ya to meet. He's gonna prove it all, so it's important for ya. I propose we gather in front of that coffee shop downtown, the one that's named after a duck. Be there at seven. It don't matter if it's inconvenient."

I played the recording back and checked my watch. Shortly, I started hyperventilating, scared. Closing my eyes, I imagined that a thin, fraying rope stretched out in front of me, and I was going to step out onto it. It would either break and I'd fall, or it would carry me from the edge of darkness and back to the light. I shut the cabinets and stared at the flashing answering machine. It was five in the evening. My parents and Matty would be arriving home soon. I erased Uncle Hewitt's message.

At dinner, my father stated comically that he intended to grow his hair out like a hippie, which would've shown off his receding hairline something awful.

217

Matty told him, "Dad, if you do that, you might look a little funny."

"Funny ain't so bad."

"Yes, it is, Stew," Momma disagreed.

"Not now that I'm getting older and less self-conscious."

Matty said, "You'd look dumb."

Abruptly, I changed subject. "Momma, can . . . can me and Matty go to the Canvasback Café for dessert?"

She looked at my dad then me. "We were talking about hair."

"I know."

"Well, how do you feel?"

"Good."

She pushed her plate away. "Sure. You should."

So, a little while later, tromping toward downtown, me and Matty played an idiotic form of tag he likes. When I was just a kid, he designed a new version of the game so that both of us could take turns being it. The rule is, at the end of every block, a person has to surrender and get touched. Mostly, we just end up chasing each other so that I get sick of playing.

Two blocks before Washington Street, feeling edgy, I told him I was done.

"Already?"

"Yeah. It's too cold and hurts my lungs."

"It hurts my lungs, too, but I wanna keep going."

"That's 'cause you don't know what's good for you."

Matty snapped back, "I know what's good for me."

"Matty, I don't mean it in a bad way. It's a saying. I was saying a saying. It's like the way people talk about how it rains cats and dogs, but it really doesn't. See?"

"Well, I know what's good for me. I'm not so stupid, Penn."

"I know you're not."

On St. John Street, we passed beside boarded doorways and thrift shops displaying shelves of empty cookie tins alongside doll babies with their hair falling out. We scooted past my grandparents' old hardware store and Totally Cowboy's broad window, where we stopped cold. Tacked to a sheet of plyboard was a reproduction pair of the biggest blue jeans ever made. The sign alongside them said the guy who'd worn the real things had needed to be buried in a piano case, which got me to wondering what a piano case looked like.

"Matty, you ever heard of a piano case?"

"I got a suitcase."

"Same here."

He asked, "Why'd they make those pants?"

"For an overweight guy to fill 'em."

"A real person?"

"That's what it says. Somebody made him his own blue jeans."

Minutes later, I spotted the Canvasback Café, where Uncle Hewitt stood outside rocking back and forth in a feeble effort to stay warm. I whispered, "Matty, before dessert, we gotta talk to Uncle Hewitt."

"He sometimes smells."

"Maybe he won't tonight," I said, wondering how my brother, who practically wears Burger King cologne, could talk about someone else's odor.

"Boys," Uncle Hewitt greeted us, steam rising from out of a paper coffee cup.

"Hey." I shifted back and forth and felt strange and skeptical of him.

He jutted a sharp elbow at me. "We're waiting for a fella named Colin Turnbull. He's another Pygmy, an important one who don't drink and lives respectfully." Hewitt's eyes got watery, and he pitched forward and coughed before wiping his nose on his windbreaker. "He's . . . he's from New York, not the city but the state. Lives in the capital, Albany. He's a scientist, not that it matters to ya. Anyways, yesterday I called him on the phone. Got him curious, so's he wanted to talk with ya."

Hewitt flattened his slicked-down hair. "Let's us go walking, get the blood moving so we don't freeze."

220

"Shouldn't we wait?"

"Colin'll find us, Penrod. He's a Pygmy, don't forget."

Matty said, "What about dessert?"

"We'll come back," I assured him.

Washington Avenue was busier than normal. Drunks were exiting out of bars, staggering for their homes or fetching bashed cars so they could race off somewhere. A few couples walked by holding hands and being romantic, while, off in the weedy area by the water, a pack of mutts yipped happily, like they'd come across a dinosaur bone.

Uncle Hewitt sipped at the dregs of his coffee. Before crossing the street at the end of the block, he crumpled the cup and deposited it in a wire trashcan. In the middle of the intersection, he started talking. "I know ya gotta be skeptical, but, here and now, Penrod, I'm saying you're an amazing boy with amazing potential. Colin and I been talking 'bout ya a lot. We have no doubt you're special."

Lowering my head, I rested my chin on my chest.

"Penrod, it can be a hard process, Pygmy Syndrome. Some say it's a privilege to hear people's private ideas, but it's a curse that can make ya feel like a rich man and a bum. No matter, we all got to overcome our issues and go on. You'll overcome yers and, one day, I have no doubt, you'll be the new king, the king of the Pygmies. That's me and Colin's prediction. Ya got that kind of greatness in ya."

Voice shaky, I said, "I don't even know how to drive, yet, Uncle Hewitt. Did you know that? I'd wreck a car."

"Penrod, there're places in the world where babies become president. People get in over their heads everywhere. Besides, ya got time." He lifted his watery eyes and looked north along Washington Street. Far off, car lights arched over the Route 40 Bridge similar to fire flies tracing a rainbow.

"What's going on?" Matty asked.

"Just conversation," I explained.

Uncle Hewitt fumbled in a pocket, found a pack of cigarettes. When he connected the lighter flame, he unintentionally lit the middle section of his smoke so that, after a minute, an uncooked inch of the tip fell off. "Penrod, ya got power that ain't been round for years."

The three of us arrived at the end of the road, stopped, circled, and shambled back along Washington Street, toward the Canvasback Café.

"Ya got big pants to wear. Colin, he's gonna monitor your progress. Top of that, he'll send down other Pygmies to get ya on the right page and understanding things."

"Uncle Hewitt, why isn't he here yet?"

He raised his eyebrows. "Don't be like your mother, Penrod. He's coming." He sucked hard at his cigarette, and the tip turned an angry, blazing orange.

Matty looked at him. "Uncle Hewitt?"

"Yeah, Matthew?"

"How about dessert?"

"Let's go on in and get some. Heck, I'm nearly frozen like a Popsicle."

I followed behind them, wishing and wishing for Colin to show. I'd never wanted something so ferociously, not even Daisy. A couple of cars rumbled past. In the sky, amongst the scattered and glistening stars, a prop plane whined like a toy, but nothing deposited the scientist from Albany.

Without waiting on me, Matty and Uncle Hewitt roamed into Canvasback's. I stopped and took some long, stabilizing breaths in the freezing air. Sensing someone approaching from behind, I turned. A local man lumbered past. I leaned against an abandoned building and tried to rid my head of hopes. I couldn't.

I went into Canvasback's, got a Coke, and sat down in a chair next to Matty and Uncle Hewitt. Matty had gotten his usual—three enormous chocolate chip cookies, one of which he'd gnawed in two parts. Already, his face was dotted with crumbs.

Uncle Hewitt was busy spiking his coffee with a tiny plastic bottle of booze. I got an odd look from him. "He's coming, Penrod. Ya gotta have faith in what ya believe or ya don't have nothing."

I nodded and sipped.

Matty said, "Uncle Hewitt, who's your favorite basketball player?"

"Of all time?"

"Yeah."

"Bob Cousy. Was a guard who played for the Celtics in the 1960s. Man was he something. Could pass the ball behind his back or throw it off the floor and it'd go right where he wanted."

"You like any new players?"

"Yeah, that big guy down in Florida."

"Shaquille O'Neal?"

"Saw him on a hamburger commercial." Uncle Hewitt slurped loudly at his coffee. "Thing is, don't take no skill to slam the ball in the basket if you're nine feet tall. I mostly root for the shorties. I like 'em. Cousy was a shorty."

Matty made a cookie disappear.

I looked at my uncle and a little too harshly asked, "Right now, what am I thinking?"

"Ya wanna meet Colin. Nothing more, nothing less."

I put a hand on the table. "There's more. I'm thinking more."

He reached around the collar of his shirt and scratched. "You're thinking that ya don't know about any or alla this."

I hunched forward. "I'm thinking that you were a happy person till Birdy died."

"Was just about to say that."

I swallowed the lump that rose in my throat. I knew none of it was real but kept my feelings inside, strumming my nearly unmanageable disappointment. "You know," I mumbled, just to talk, "it used to be that I took everything for granted. I figured I'd go off to college and get a degree in something, but I didn't know what. I didn't especially like anything a whole lot. Now it's different. I like town and the way I live. I like my friends and my family, and I got a girlfriend. I don't wanna lose any of it."

Uncle Hewitt said, "You're human. Course ya don't wanna lose your way of life. But ain't nothing can be taken that ya don't give. I didn't hand over a thing till I lost my Birdy. I had a good existence."

I could hardly look at him. "Do you really hear voices?"

He nodded. "All of them telling things about this and that and the way people are. It's . . . it's people's secret thoughts."

"Really, Uncle Hewitt?"

He put his coffee cup on the shiny table. "Penrod, be strong. It's what'll carry ya through. It ain't a great pleasure ride. A Pygmy can't ever live without being on high alert and making sure that folks around him are talking or not talking, but that's the way it goes. You gotta appreciate smaller happinesses more than regular folk."

"Do you watch people's lips?"

"Used to. I can mostly tell who and when someone's actually yammering now. The only person I ever let my guard down around was Birdy, and . . . I guess, you. Birdy, she used to joke me 'cause I talked to myself so much. I always been able to hold conversations with my head. Sometimes, Birdy'd ask me what people was saying. Sometimes, she'd ask me to tell her 'bout the history of Pygmies. Was all entertaining for her. I'd say how Napoleon was one and that Sammy Davis Jr. was the same way. She loved hearing that stuff, 'cause I knew the history and she didn't."

Matty said, "Who's Sammy Davis Jr.?" like he hadn't heard any other part of our conversation.

Uncle Hewitt made a fist and touched his chest. "Sammy Davis Jr. Oh, Matty, he was a special man, an entertainer extraordinaire. Looked funny as you'd ever guess, what with being a tiny black man with straight hair and a long nose. But that guy could play a crowd like nobody's business."

Curious and far-away feeling, I asked, "Are there any other Pygmy stars?"

"Sure. You know Dustin Hoffman?"

I didn't.

"You know that small actor, that Cruise fella who's always breaking up with his wife?"

"Tom Cruise?"

Uncle Hewitt grinned. "Mark my word, Tommy Cruise is a Pygmy. I seen it in his eye, Penrod."

"He must be a really powerful one."

"Oh, he is. But! But he can't match you. You're doing stuff ain't nobody but the kings ever done. You're exclusive."

"I wanna be."

"You don't gotta wanna."

I sucked at my Coke and placed my hands on the tabletop in order to crack each knuckle. Time passed slowly, like algebra class. Matty began telling Uncle Hewitt Burger King stories, which got them both laughing like hysterics. Our uncle especially liked the time Matty tripped over an enormous green bucket of pickles and put his hand flat on the char broiler. It didn't take a genius to figure out why Matty's hard-to-follow adventures were tickling Uncle Hewitt so well, though. For an hour, he'd been increasing the percentage of alcohol to coffee in his cup. Already, he had finished two little bottles of booze and had commenced on a third.

I got up and wiped down Matty's face.

Matty hardly noticed.

At nine, the owners of Canvasback's began closing their store down. They locked the front door and started sweeping and wiping tables. Uncle Hewitt took note and swigged what remained in his cup. Abruptly, he rose from his chair. Stretching, he declared, "Guess Colin got held up somewheres. Oh, well. I'll talk to him later, see why he didn't show."

Matty stood, too.

I kept my seat like I was glued to it. "We aren't actually leaving, are we?"

"Done waiting, Penrod."

I shook my head. I didn't want the evening to end that way. The next day, I would see Dr. Fjord, and I wanted solid ground to stand on when I announced myself sane. My hands balled into fists and my jaw tightened. "That's it, you're just quitting?"

"Can't do nothing if a man don't show."

I scooted out my chair. "Can we wait outside?"

"Naw. Too cold on the sidewalk."

Slowly, I got the hard-to-shake desire to pummel Uncle Hewitt. I could feel the slim, tight rope beneath my feet give way and my body drift down, down, down, toward the rocks below. "Uncle Hewitt, I need to know!" The remaining customers in Canvasback's looked at me. "I need to know if we're real."

Uncle Hewitt grinned at me. "Do ya?" He pointed a knobby finger. "It's your job to show people ya are." He gave an exasperated breath and shuffled forward, bent and cupped a hand to my ear. "Penrod, here it is. Listen up. Ya gotta believe enough to get ya by. That's all that matters. Ain't no amount of evidence gonna prove it if ya don't have a tiny bit of faith."

"Faith?"

Chapter Nineteen

That night, I didn't go to sleep right off. I couldn't. I was feeling too swindled.

In a strange stupor, I sat at my desk and thought about everything that had happened earlier and everything that hadn't, and I kept coming back to Uncle Hewitt saying I gotta believe enough to get by.

I shuffled over to my bed and sat on the edge scared to death. I considered my fifth-grade science teacher, who'd been nice even when he dressed in barbwire clothing. He'd gone off to a hospital for help and returned like a fly drained of life, like nothing but a crispy body. I didn't want to be that way.

I flopped sideways, my head crashing into my pillow. In the gray light, I moved my fingers so that they flickered like a nest of snakes. Everything was a mistake. I was too average and young to get stuck with such a shitty problem.

Woozy with fatigue and unhappiness, my mind began to drift. Then, just before I fell asleep, I thought of Matty, cool, handsome Matty, and I felt a little lighter. His exterior was fine, but his brain had troubled spots. In a weird way, we were similar.

In the morning, the weak fall sun glinted in the padded sky like a salt-corroded piece of metal. Confused, I lifted off my drooled-on pillow and glanced toward the clock on my dresser. It took a moment for my eyes to focus, and, when they did, I felt my insides drop like a sack of dirt rolled off a wall. It was almost time for school, and I hadn't told Daisy the truth about what was happening. If I went into a hospital, she'd head to class alone, eat lunch alone, and leave for home alone, maybe for weeks, and she'd never know where I'd gotten to.

In a rush, I got dressed and hurtled down the stairs, stopping when I got to the kitchen.

"What are you doing?" Momma asked from her spot beside the counter.

Dad and Matty watched me from the table.

"I'll be back."

Momma lowered the front page of the newspaper.

"I gotta tell Daisy where I might be," I explained, exiting out the side entrance of our house and whipping the door closed behind me. I shot along the driveway and up the sidewalk, running fast. On Revolution Street, I headed west, weaving around other students as they made their way to class.

Near school, I circled back toward Daisy's condominium, tracing the route we'd taken when I'd walked her home. I crossed the street between cars and was jogging when I spotted her ahead, her book bag over her shoulder. Even from a distance, I could see her sharp-creased secretary pants cutting the air like side-by-side sails.

I slowed and caught my breath. I waved and she waved back.

When she got closer, she said, "What are you doing here?"

I told her, "I'm sick but don't feel bad."

She was confused.

"I'm mentally ill, maybe. That's a fact. I wasn't gonna tell you."

She stopped.

"Daisy, I'm going to a doctor, and he'll tell me I'm a goner 'cause I hear voices in my head. I hear them like conversations."

Her face seemed unstuffed of bones and muscles. "Penn, you aren't mentally ill."

"I talk to myself."

"I do too."

"But I hear words in my head."

"Everybody does."

"Not like me."

She got her arms from her pack and dropped it to the sidewalk. Blank-faced, she checked her watch.

I told her, "I know you gotta get to class."

"Just say what's happening first."

I admitted, "I might be schizophrenic some. That's what people think."

She poked at her glasses. "Not really?"

"Really."

She breathed in and out slowly, her nostrils barely flaring like they do. "You don't seem it."

In the street, a car with a bad muffler boomed by. Dizzy, I whispered, "I don't wanna be."

Daisy reached and held one of my hands. "What do the voices say?"

"They just talk. Sometimes it seems like a lot are going. Sometimes it's just a single person. I ignore them mostly. Mostly, it's just confusing, 'cause, at first they fooled me into thinking I was experiencing a miracle. It seemed like I heard what was going on in people's heads."

Daisy said, "Penn, the other day, by the water, it

233

seemed like you were reading my mind. You told me mostly what I was thinking."

Uncle Hewitt's Pygmy stories whirled about in my thoughts. "Really?"

"Yes."

"I'm glad. I'm glad to know," I said softly, relieved that we both cared for each other equally.

Quiet fell over us like shaken-out dust, then Daisy said, "You know Joan of Arc? I read about her last year. She heard voices, and she's a saint. In the Middle Ages, she led the French against the English and became a hero. She thought God talked to her, but doctors now think she was unstable."

"She heard voices?"

"Yeah, and she saved France."

"Was she short?"

"I don't know."

I considered things, and said, "I gotta go tell Momma about Joan."

Daisy laughed. "Her name's Joan of Arc. If you call her Joan, your mother won't know who you're talking about."

"Joan of Arc," I said. "Joan of Arc. I gotta tell her."

"Will you call me?"

"You still want me to?"

"While I'm in Havre de Grace."

I waited a moment before saying, "You can change your mind."

"I won't." Daisy stepped toward me, so that our stomachs touched. "You're fine," she said, and kissed my cheek. "Don't let them say you aren't."

I touched my head to hers. "Maybe I'll let them say what they want, and I'll just know. Maybe that's what I should do."

"Maybe," she said, and I was suddenly sure that, years before, Aunt Birdy had told Uncle Hewitt the same thing. And, finally, I understood what my uncle had intended. I'd been facing a terrible reality, and he'd offered me an alternative.

I walked Daisy partway to school, stopped and watched her reach the corner of Congress Avenue. We waved, and she was gone, heading for class. Already lonely for her voice and smell, I started back home, shivering so that my shoulders must've looked like the loose hood on my father's truck. Above, the sky resembled a rolled out blanket of partially used cotton, like it'd been sitting at the bottom of a dirty closet. On Union Avenue, I passed the fancy bed-and-breakfast hotels and Havre de Grace Hospital, with its out-of-place double-decker garage. Far ahead, I could see Millard Tydings Park, a greenish-brown line where the street ended.

I went up our walkway and in through the front door, wondering what I was going to say to Momma, who I knew was alone since Dad's truck was gone.

Momma called, "Penn?" from the kitchen.

I shuffled through the empty dining room to where she sat at the breakfast table across from the kitchen sink, her coffee mug near one of her hands. "Hey."

"Hey."

"You probably thought I was running away."

"I didn't."

I pulled out a chair and sat.

Her expression didn't change.

"Momma?" I said.

"Yes."

"Can I talk and you listen?"

She nodded.

"Don't yell."

"I never yell."

"Well, don't get upset, I mean. 'Cause I've been thinking and thinking that I don't want help for my problem. I want to stay who I am right now. I'm okay with it."

She didn't answer.

"I don't wanna be treated like I'm sick when I enjoy my life."

Her eyes narrowed. "Realistically, how long can you continue to enjoy it?"

I thought about her question. "I don't know. But, for me, maybe doing something would be worse than doing nothing?"

"Think about the last few weeks, Penrod. How can you say that?"

I tipped forward in my chair. "Momma, it caught me by surprise, but it won't anymore. Uncle Hewitt sort of helped with that."

She put an elbow on the table and rested her chin on a turned up palm. "How could he possibly help with anything? He's lost touch and isn't sure what's real and what's not, even if he did know once."

"I think he knows."

Momma lowered her hand, her mouth drawn tight. "He doesn't, and you need to recognize that what you're experiencing makes you susceptible to his tall tales. I wish I could tell you differently, but I can't."

"Do you think people said that to Joan of Arc? She probably didn't get any special mental care, and she saved France. Sometimes, letting a person hear voices must be okay."

Momma smiled. "Joan of Arc?"

"She heard voices."

"These days, she would've been medicated."

"She became a saint."

"It doesn't matter."

I smacked the table. "You always gotta try and fix things, no matter what?"

"That's what psychiatrists are trained to do."

"God, Momma, who cares? What's so bad about playing you're a Pygmy? It's not a crime."

"It's delusional, Penn. Why would you even argue?" She glared hard. "I know you're frightened, but—"

"I'm not. Except for having to see Dr. Fjord, I'm fine."

Momma's glare didn't falter. "He lacks a bedside manner, but he's got the best reputation in the area."

"I don't need his reputation to tell me things." I waited for that to sink in and continued. "Momma, tell me the truth. Do you think Uncle Hewitt has been this way since he was a teenager?"

"I couldn't even guess. It might be that he doesn't know himself."

"Do you think he's had it since he was my age?"

She shook her head. "He made it sound like Aunt Birdy knew the situation, and I'd bet she did. It's very likely she's why he was able to hide it for so long."

"Still, he did okay," I said. "He might've thought he was a Pygmy, but that didn't stop him from becoming the police chief. Last night he told me . . ."

Momma interrupted. "You saw him last night?"

"Me and Matty talked to him."

"My God, Penn, do I have to get a restraining order against him?"

"Listen for now, okay? You said you'd let me talk."

"But he's twisting you up inside. It's dangerous."

I snapped, "What's so dangerous about it? Can you tell me so I understand? He knows Pygmy Syndrome isn't real. He knows."

Clamping her jaw tight and standing, Momma wandered over to the sink. She filled a glass with tap water and lingered there. "Penn, you're my normal boy."

I mumbled, "That's what I want to be."

"It would be negligent. Schizophrenia can be devastating. Plus, it very well could be something else. We don't know."

I answered, "It's not anything else, Momma. I got a light case, like Uncle Hewitt. I can ignore it. I'm good at ignoring."

She watched me closely. "A professional needs to make a diagnosis."

"I'll get a diagnosis, but when we have one, let me be me for a while. I wanna try."

Momma put her water glass on the counter without taking a sip. "Penn, all I've ever wanted for my children was happiness. That's always been my dream. If life had unwound like it should have, I could promise you and Matty that the future can be as bright and clear as you make it. Now I can't. Circumstances cloud everything. That's devastating."

I leaned against the table. "Momma, Matty's the happiest person I know. That's not so bad."

She smiled sadly.

"I just wanna chance."

"You see how Uncle Hewitt ended up?"

"But I'm different. I'm okay."

She concentrated on the sink bottom and dabbed a hand against her runny nostrils. "I'm thinking, okay? I'm thinking about how to save my normal boy."

"Say we can try."

She looked over a shoulder at me. She looked and blinked and looked some more. "We can try."

Sometime after that, I went upstairs, stripped down, and got into the shower. When I was done, I dripped across the bathroom mat and the white floor tiles. At the sink, I stood in front of the foggy mirror and wiped the steam away. Rising on my toes to get close, I was caught by surprise. I had three new whiskers. I pushed on them with a finger and rotated my head sideways.

A towel around me, I scampered to my room and

took hold of my penknife. I unfolded the blade, then got to the floor and screeched my damp shoulders under Granddad Penrod's colorfully historic bed. Delicately, I carved a line separate from the others to represent the first morning I was new-normal.

Getting up, I slipped into a T-shirt. When my arms and head were through, I found myself facing the poster of the man stepping out of a window into thin air. In a way, Momma was allowing me to do the same thing.

I looked off through my own window, toward the Chesapeake Bay, which resembled a fine polished silver tray reflecting the huge white sky. Beyond it, over the far shoreline, a dark gray cloud hung like a stone wall. As soon as I saw it, huge and powerful, I thought about how I'd always been good at ignoring things that weren't likely to change. My hometown has given me that gift.

Havre de Grace is a rugged, ancient place with un-predictable weather and a long history that includes the chapter in which my uncle was a famous police chief who could talk any violent person into surrendering without a hitch. I know how he did it, too. He is a Pygmy, and I am a Pygmy King. We read minds. Of course, we have to keep our existence and heightened mental abilities secret from most everyone. We can't let the government find out. But over the months since my talent interrupted my life, it has taught me something that Daisy, Momma, and Dad should know and that Matty already understands. On the other side of hard luck, miracles and hope can exist, even in a town like Havre de Grace.

Author's Note

When I originally wrote *King of the Pygmies* and its accompanying author's note, I felt very good about what I had produced. The end of the novel is hopeful but also frightening and fraught with possible complications—just like life. I didn't write the ending this way because I believe psychotropic drugs to be dangerous or because I believed mental illness a dilemma that one can, by force of will, control—I especially do not think that. I wrote it for a myriad of reasons, the most important being my own familiarity with the internal decisions and issues Penn faced.

Until recently, I've never told anyone other than my family and a few friends that I am bipolar, that I experience severe and debilitating mood swings that change almost every aspect of my personality. But since the publication of *King of the Pygmies,* I have had the good luck to work with various mental health organizations, and from those experiences and others, I have decided to come forward about the fact that I have a severe mental illness.

I experienced my first bout of depression at the age of twelve. During that time, I grew dangerously despondent, morose, deeply confused, and, worst of all, I felt as if I'd lost all control of my life. About a year later, when the illness retreated to a dull whine in my head, I believed that my future had already been taken away by something I had no influence over, something that would visit again.

In my college years, I continued to believe myself ruined by my problems. Year after year, I broke like glass. After graduation, I struggled with who I was. Sometimes, I enjoyed a sudden jolt of energy and intellect. I was funny, quick. That would change into an unfocused fury and disgust. At that point, I feared the overwhelming blackness that I knew was next. It would leave me unable to think, to speak, to see any good at all. Then, weeks later, that too was gone, and I'd settle into a relatively normal routine, telling myself that I would never go through such a horrible assault of emotions again. I always did.

All the while, I wrote. I loved writing, and I believe it saved me by giving me control over a small fictional world. I needed to have some control, as I believe Penn would. I also felt that writing is a way in which I can contribute to the world, by dealing with issues I feel strongly about. Regardless, back then I wasn't medicated, and left untreated, a severe mental illness can tear a person apart, which is what it started doing to me. That experience motivated me not to romanticize Penn's problems but to place the reader inside his head. I wanted to show what Penn might feel, how a normal boy's entire worldview might shift, how much he could hang on to the notion of blind hope. I wanted to leave the reader with the feeling that Penn's life would eventually become a dance with the devil and that, medicated or not, he would always be capable of exerting some force of will and control over his partner.

For me, my illness can be inexplicably misleading and destructive, utterly confusing, and frequently alarming. And most bipolar disorders are not as bad as schizophrenia, which, in its moderate to severe forms, is nearly overwhelming. Still, after the publication of *King of the Pygmies,* I am often asked if I have any personal experiences with the disease. In these questions I've come to see how people with problems seek to know they're not alone, that their future hasn't been stolen from them. When my personal story or my books provide someone with that hope, I'm always touched and amazed.

As of this printing, I have been on psychotropic drugs for fourteen years. I don't believe that I'd be alive without them. But there is a human component to all mental health problems that is too easily forgotten in this age of lithium and Prozac. Healthy or not, all of us must believe that we are the exclusive owners of the light that is who we are inside our souls. We can't wholly count on pharmaceuticals for that job, or else the human part of us disappears.

Finally, in order to depict Penn's state of mind, I reflected on my own history. Sometimes it hasn't been very attractive. Sometimes it hasn't been pleasant. Frequently, I've wondered how I made it to this point. That's when I am forced to admit to myself that I've leaned heavily on others during good portions of my difficult journey. During other parts, I stumbled forward alone. But I have gotten this far. I trust that Penn takes strength in that. In fact, I hope his own difficult passage touches and informs the hearts and minds of both the sick and the well, which was and remains my aspiration for *King of the Pygmies.*

In closing, I need to thank the people without whom this book would not have been written.

First, there is psychiatric social worker extraordinaire, Daniel Buccino, co-director of the Baltimore Psychotherapy Institute and a faculty member of the Johns Hopkins University School of Medicine. On our many jogs around the city of Baltimore, he gave me multiple answers to my scattershot questions about the disease, its effects, and its many manifestations. He was always very patient.

Additionally, I appreciate the help of Swaran Dhawan, a highly regarded psychiatric social worker from Taylor Manor Hospital who worked with schizo-phrenics for many years. She enthusiastically helped me understand the horror, humor, and humanity experi-enced by the disease's varied sufferers. For so many rea-sons, I thank her deeply.

Dr. Joseph (Joe) Bierman, a noted child and adoles-cent psychiatrist, was also indispensable. Confused by my research, I frequently phoned Joe at all hours of the day and night. Joe not only responded quickly to my dif-ficult questions but also proffered precise medical refer-ences as well as an abundance of general reference materials. Without Joe, I would've been up a creek.

Certainly, I would be remiss if I didn't thank Liz Bicknell, my long-suffering editor, who patiently sent me back to the drawing board till the book achieved what I truly intended. She kept a steady hand on the tiller, and I appreciate that more than she knows.

Last but far from least, I thank my family, all of whom consistently put up with far too much from me. Daily, I thank them for their kindness, inspiration, and joy.

If you or anyone in your family suffers from any of the symptoms mentioned above, please search the multiple resources within your community for answers to your questions or concerns, or simply contact the National Alliance for the Mentally Ill at www.nami.org

or 1-800-950-NAMI. They can provide a range of resources, from national to local diagnostic information, and treatment suggestions. Finally, it should be noted that the majority of psychiatrists are not like the one portrayed in *King of the Pygmies*. Most are kind, thoughtful, and want nothing more than to aid and comfort those afflicted by mental illness. Do not fear them.

—Jonathon Scott Fuqua